TRAVIS

THE GRIM SINNER'S MOTORYCGLE CLUB

LeAnn Ashers

Copyright

Designer: Regina Wamba

Photographer: Wander Aquilar

Editor: Stephanie Marshall Ward at Eats, Shoots, Edits

Formatter: Brenda Wright, Formatting Done Wright

Table of Contents

prologue

I never expected to get pregnant at seventeen and have a daughter at eighteen.

When you are young you have this perfect life in your head, and I thought I had already found *the one* and would be happy forever. But the guy who had gotten me pregnant was not the man I thought he was.

Adeline came into my life when I needed her most. I was lost and so confused about what to do with my life, but I knew I wanted a fresh start. I wanted my daughter to live in a world different from the one I'd grown up in.

At the age of twenty-one, I was struggling big time to support myself and my daughter. My mother had kicked me out of the house when she found out I was pregnant, and my boyfriend did not want me. He'd felt obligated to help, so he'd rented me a one-bedroom apartment and only paid one month's rent. That was the first and only time he ever helped me do anything.

I worked three jobs and managed to save enough money to live on for a while after Gabby was born; then I went to school to become a makeup artist. But now, due to the high cost of living in Hawaii, I was struggling more than ever, and I wanted a fresh start somewhere new. That's when I met Adeline, who gave me the strength to get out and be my own person again. She also gave me hope that I would not be completely alone, so it wasn't so scary. Who knew doing one person's makeup would completely change my life?

one

Bailey

As we get off the plane, Smiley helps us with our stuff. We're disembarking from a private jet, mind you, which completely blows my mind. I help Gabby walk down the steps. She's half asleep and has trouble balancing on her little legs. She slept throughout the plane ride, and it took me a while to wake her up. She is a really heavy sleeper.

We walk across the lot to two parked SUVs. A big man—as tall as Smiley—is talking to Smiley and Adeline. They look at me, and the guy turns around. His eyes widen when he sees me; then it's like he trips on air. He grabs the side of the SUV to keep himself from hitting the ground.

Hmm, that was weird. I look down at my daughter, who is grinning like this is the most common thing in the world. "I guess you're my ride?" I ask the guy. My face is burning and I know it's red.

He clears his throat. "Yeah." He opens the door and I see a car seat strapped into the back seat. "Oh, thank you for the seat!"

He blushes before my very eyes. The most gorgeous man I have ever seen in my life is blushing at my compliment. He shakes his head like he is trying to clear his thoughts and bends down to Gabby's level. "Can I help you into your seat, doll?" He smiles at her and she returns it. She goes straight to him, and he lifts her into the SUV and buckles her in like a pro. He opens the passenger door for me, which completely shocks me for some reason.

I look back at Gabby, who is still holding the doll Adeline gave her. Sadly, Gabby has not had the privilege of having many people in her life besides me and the babysitter. Her dad sure wasn't in the picture, and my mother doesn't even admit she ever had a daughter. My mother is all about her public image, and if anyone hinders that, even a little bit, they are pushed away and forgotten.

Instead of being ashamed, my mother should have protected me. The guy who got me pregnant when I was seventeen was thirty-five years old, and I didn't even know it. I am sickened that he was so much older and, in a way, I feel foolish because I was played by him. He told me whatever I wanted to hear, and he played me like a fiddle.

The driver's door opens and my driver gets inside. I am hit with his warm and woodsy smell, which is all man and makes him ten times sexier in my eyes. He is a very attractive man. His hair is cut short, and the top is gelled and combed slightly to the side. His body, from what I can see, is a work of art. He is big and muscular, and his brawny arms are tattooed down to his wrists. I clear my throat, and he looks at me and smiles slightly. Oh boy, he is a lady-killer for sure.

"Mommy, can I have a shake?" Gabby is holding her doll and looking around the SUV. I am not sure what to say. I don't have my own vehicle.

"Sure, sweetheart," Travis says, surprising me.

"You don't have to." I don't want him to feel obligated to do that.

He shakes his head, smiling. "It's nothing, the princess is wanting a milkshake and fries?" He winks at her.

She giggles. "Wight."

I laugh. My daughter is a little angel. She came into my life when I needed her the most; I felt so alone in this world. She gave me something to push me through, and I wanted to better myself—for her. She is my whole world. "What do you say, baby?" I tell her.

"Thank you," she says in her cute little baby voice.

He laughs. "You are welcome, sweetheart. What does Momma want?" He looks at me from the corner of his eye.

I bite my lip to stop myself from groaning at hearing him call me *Momma*. I don't know why, but that got to me a bit. My stomach is twisting. "Hmm." I press my hand against my face. "I think a double cheeseburger with the works, some fries, and a chocolate shake." My mouth is watering at the idea; the plane ride was long, and I am in dire need of some greasy, not-good-for-me food.

"A woman after my heart." He can't say that to a woman. She might never be the same after that. Hell, I don't think I will be the same after just being in his presence.

"I can already see that it's so different here from Hawaii." I look at the buildings and the people on the streets, waving to us as we pass.

"I bet it was nice to live in Hawaii, though."

He is right. Hawaii is beautiful, but it was not my home. Home is not a virtual prison cell that brought years of stress and aggravation. "Being so close to the beach was nice."

He pulls over into a diner parking lot. It looks like it's straight from the movie *Grease*, which I have seen so many times. "How cute," I tell him, and he smiles and gets out of the SUV.

Bless my heart, he is so pretty it should be a crime. Hell, there should at least be a warning label so we can brace ourselves. Most of the guys I have seen surrounding Adeline are out-of-this-world gorgeous. Her man, Smiley, is a silver fox and is a downright sin to look at. One thing is for certain: he is so in love with her. The way he looks at her is something straight out of a book. I hope that someday I will have a smidge of that. What would it be like to be in love with someone and have them love you back?

I know one thing: I will not settle unless I have what Adeline and Smiley have. It would not be fair to myself. I have had a shitty enough time, and I don't need another man like my ex.

I do want Gabby to have a father figure in her life, someone to look up to, but I can be both her mother and father. I have done that from the moment she was born.

I had her alone, though the hospital nurses kept me from feeling lonely. My mother did not even call me, and my ex only showed up to sign the birth certificate. Then Gabby came, and I knew I would never be alone again.

I wish my ex hadn't shown up at all; he only came around to torture me. He would bring food for himself and eat it at my house, when he knew that I hadn't eaten in two days. Hawaii was not cheap, and Gabby's needs always came first. I did everything completely alone, and I am damn proud of myself. No matter how hard it got, I was up every single morning and did what I could to provide and care for my daughter.

In the diner parking lot, I open my door and climb out before I get too lost in my thoughts. Travis surprises me again by unbuckling Gabby from her seat and helping her out.

"Fank you." She smiles at him and grabs my hand.

"Thank you," I say. "You don't have to help me. You know that, right?"

He shakes his head. "It's a habit. There are a lot of kids in the MC, and we want to make it easier on the women when we are around." He winks as he walks past me. I hold my chest. *Oh boy.*

"Can I hold his hand?" Gabby asks.

Wait, what? She has never asked to do something like that before. I look at Travis.

"Whatever the princess wants."

Yeah. They need to grow more of him, so I can have one for myself. Gabby shakes my hand off and grabs his. His hand swallows hers, and it's so cute. She is so tiny compared to him. I lick my lips. There is nothing sexier than seeing a man being such a sweetheart to a kid.

Travis

Fuck me, I am in so much trouble. The moment I saw her step off the plane and walk toward me, I almost fell on my ass.

Bailey is fucking tiny but out-of-this-world gorgeous. Her dark brown hair flowing all around her. Her big eyes, the way they caught my eye and stared right into my fucking soul. Then I saw she had a daughter. Fuck me, she is the spitting image of her mother. The mother is a sweetheart, and her little girl is already stealing my heart. Is it weird that I know that she is going to be mine? I never knew what my brothers were talking about until I saw her. I just knew.

We sit down and I hand Bailey and Gabby menus.

"I don't need that, I want some pancakes." Gabby has her hand up. I laugh because she sounds so grown up.

Bailey blushes. "Don't be rude, baby."

"I was not, I was speaking my thoughts."

I laugh again. "She is right, Momma." Her face reddens. Oh, yeah. I am going to love every fucking minute of chasing her and capturing all of her. I want to see how far that blush goes. And her daughter is so cute; she is a mini version of her mom.

"I fink I like it here." Gabby looks out the window at the traffic.

"I am glad, sweet girl." Bailey smooths down her hair. She is a good mom. I can tell by the way she stares at her daughter like the world begins and ends with her.

The waitress comes over, and we give her our orders.

"Play on your phone?" Gabby asks her mom.

"I am sorry, baby, my phone is dead."

I reach into my pocket and take out my phone. "Here, you can play with mine." Her eyes light up and she slips under the table. She peeks at me, and I touch the top of her head so she doesn't bump it. She climbs into the seat with me and reaches her small hands out for my phone. I click on Netflix Kids. I look at Bailey to make sure she is okay with everything, and she is smiling.

"You just made a best friend for life. You know, she has always been kind of wary of guys, but with you it seems that went completely out the window." Well, that feels fucking amazing.

Our food arrives a few minutes later. I take Gabby's plate and immediately start cutting up her pancakes for her.

"You don't have to do that, I can do it," Bailey says.

I shake my head. "Rest. You had a long trip, and I know you are exhausted." She really does look tired. The trip from Hawaii was long, and I know she is mentally drained from having to move her life.

"Thank you, Travis." She smiles and takes a huge bite out of her burger. I love a woman with an appetite, especially one that looks like her.

I help Gabby with her food; she is sitting on her knees so she can reach the table. She is inhaling it. I grab my own burger and eat.

"Ahh! My hands." Gabby has put her hands in her plate, which is now covered in pancake syrup.

"Gabby." Bailey laughs and takes a pack of baby wipes from her purse. I take the wipes from her. Gabby giggles when her fingers start sticking together.

"Let me see your hands, angel." She thrusts them in my direction, still giggling. I clean her hands.

"You are good with kids," Bailey says.

"My cousin Wilder has a little baby, and we all pitch in to help each other. These little munchkins are the most important things in our lives."

"All of you guys are like a huge family, aren't you?"

I nod. "Yes, some of us may not be blood, but we are a family. Family does not mean blood, it's the people you are close to."

She smiles. "I love that. That's the way it should be."

I don't know what to say to her, so I nod. Smiley told me she doesn't have any family. We set up one of our rental houses for Bailey; it's actually next to mine. Since she is new in town, we thought she would feel better if she's close to people she knows. That's why I picked her up today. Gabby settles back in her seat, yawns, and lays her head on my bicep, closing her eyes.

Bailey

Okay, I can't get over how comfortable Gabby has been around Travis since the moment she met him. This has never happened before.

She has always been wary around men, since the only one she's known is her father, and he has not been around often. She is usually glued to my hip, but now she is lying against Travis's arm with her eyes closed, trying to sleep. This is wild. Travis is completely unfazed by it all; it's so natural to him. I am used to doing everything for her, but he cut up her food and cleaned her hands without thinking.

Travis breaks me out of my thoughts. "I think you are going to like your new place, it's completely remodeled."

"Thank you guys for finding me a place. You have made the move so easy."

He grins at me. "It's nothing." He's shrugging it off, but it is something. Not many people would go out of their way to do something like that.

"I have to find a job. That's the first thing I must do."

He puts his burger down. "Oh yeah, we own a salon, and you have a job there if you want it. We were wanting to expand."

What the heck? Are these people even real? "That would be amazing." I have to admit a huge part of me wants to turn it down, because I want to do it myself, but to support my daughter I will do whatever it takes. She is asleep, lying against his arm like this is the most natural thing in the world. When the check comes, I reach for it but it's snatched away from me before I can even touch it. "I can get mine and Gabby's." I wiggle my fingers for him to give me the check.

He chuckles. "I got it."

"You don't have to do that, I got it. Trust me." I start to stand and snatch it away from him, but the waitress shows up and he hands her his credit card. Really? I sit back in my seat with my arms across my chest. I am kind of pissed—I am not going to lie. I can take care of myself and my daughter.

"Bailey, I am sorry if I made you mad. Let me do something nice for you. I don't think you have had too many nice things happen to you."

Well, he hit the nail right on the head. My throat dries. I have not experienced kindness like this in such a long time. Yeah, it's just food but that shit means a lot. "Thank you, Travis." My voice is softer than usual.

His face softens and he smiles at me. "You're welcome." The waitress comes back with the check, and we stand up to leave. Gabby is still asleep. "Want me to carry her out?" Travis asks.

I hesitate before nodding. It will be much easier for him carry her than for me to wake her up. We walk out of the diner. I know I will be back; I love the atmosphere in there.

Gabby is lying against his shoulder, and I've got to admit the man has never looked better. Since I've had my daughter, seeing a guy with a small child makes my ovaries want to explode. There's nothing better than a man taking care of a child. You get to see his softer side, something men don't show a lot of people.

If only men saw that all women were once little girls. I cannot even fathom my daughter meeting a guy like her father and being treated the way I was. It took a long time for me to grow a thick enough skin to ignore everything. Going on no sleep for weeks, my ex showing up and saying I looked like absolute shit and he was thankful that he'd only had only to sleep with me a handful of times. That shit fucks with your head; that's for sure.

I want my daughter to experience a love that only happens in books. I want to press it into her brain that she will never accept less than the absolute best for herself. I want her to be independent and never, ever have to rely on someone to take care of her. I want her to never know what it's like to go without eating for a couple days, to live off of

Ramen noodles, or to drink chicken broth to fill up her stomach just a bit.

One thing I am fucking happy about is that she has never gone without a single thing she needed; she was never touched by all of this shit. I am proud of that. She is always going to have someone to support her, help her through all of her troubles, and push her to be the best she can be. My life is hers.

"What are you thinking so hard about?" I jolt and look at Travis, who is staring at me.

"Nothing." I shake my head. There is no way I would tell him all my thoughts. He stares at me for a few beats before opening the back door and setting my baby in her car seat. Her eyes open for a split second before she is out again. I laugh. "She slept on the plane ride over, but I guess she is still tired." I don't know what it's like not to be tired, so I guess this is not fazing me.

"Jet lag," Travis says. "Let me get you guys home so you can rest."

"That sounds amazing." I get into the SUV, thinking about a hot bath and a warm bed.

Wait, what am I going to do about a vehicle? Fuck, I never thought about that.

Travis turns on the radio to a country music station. Country music is my weakness—that's for sure. I know every song possible. When you can't afford a TV, you do the next best thing and listen to music.

A few minutes later we turn off on a side road; then we come to a gate. "What is this place?"

"We own a gated community."

The MC owns a gated community? "Wait, am I staying here?" I ask him.

He doesn't say a word; he just drives through the gate. I see huge houses far enough apart to provide plenty of privacy. He pulls to a stop, then into a driveway. "That is your house." He points to the house, and then he points to one next to it. "That one is mine."

I cover my mouth with my hands. *That is really mine?* "No, it's too much. I am not sure I can afford it."

"Don't worry about the rent. It's covered by the MC, and you will live here for as long as you want. Forever if you need to."

"But I don't understand...why?" This is not a normal thing that people do.

"Sweetheart, we know what it is to struggle. If we can make someone's life easier, we will. Adeline, the mom of the MC, has taken you under her wing, so that makes you family. You'll get used to it."

He gets out of the vehicle, and I stare at him through the window. Questions keep going through my mind. *Is this real?*

Gabby wakes up when Travis opens my door. As I step out of the SUV, he helps her out and she takes my hand. Travis opens the back of the vehicle and takes our bags. I open my mouth to tell him I can do that, but he shakes his head, knowing exactly what I was going to say.

I laugh and let him walk in front of us, carrying our huge suitcases—I had to push them down the stairs to get them to the car. His muscles are bulging, and my mouth dries at how sexy he looks. He sets the bags on the porch, reaches inside his pocket, and hands me a set of keys. "These are yours."

I slowly reach out and take them from him. "Thank you, Travis," I whisper and unlock the door.

Gabby and I walk inside. Travis walks in behind us and presses the buttons to disarm the alarm system. "I will give you the numbers for it in a bit."

A huge flat-screen hangs on the wall of the living room, and there's a white sectional in the corner of the room. A vase full of lilies sits on the coffee table, which is gold with a glass surface. The room is beautifully decorated in gold and white. I love it.

We walk into the kitchen. It's completely redone, and all the appliances are new. The bar in the middle of the room is white marble with gold embedded in it. Gabby lets go of my hand and opens the refrigerator, and it's fully stocked. She grabs a juice and opens it, completely comfortable here.

I lean against the counter, staring at everything. It's hard to believe this is where I will be living. I was living in a one-bedroom apartment in a horrible part of town. I went to sleep every single night scared out of my mind. Drug deals were made right downstairs, in front of the apartment complex. But my only options were to be homeless or live in that apartment; I chose the latter.

"Let me show you your rooms." We follow Travis up a flight of stairs, and he shows me my room first. Its huge and absolutely beautiful; everything is already decorated the way I would've done it. He sets my bags down inside my room; then he opens the door next to mine. I stare at Gabby's room, amazed. Gabby screams and runs to the bed, which is shaped like a carriage.

Travis laughs, and I smile at her happy face, but on the inside this shit hurts me right to the core. I wish I could have given her this a long time ago. I wish she'd had everything she wanted in life.

This just gives me a push to better myself even more. I will hustle and do whatever it takes to give her this life. My eyes burn from unshed tears as she opens a toy box full of toys. This is just too much. I turn around so she doesn't see my tears.

Travis

I can tell Bailey is overwhelmed, and I take that as my cue to leave and let her get her bearings. I don't want to go, but I will not be fucking selfish—she deserves for me to make this as easy as I can for her.

"Alright, I will let you guys get settled," I tell them both, and Gabby looks up from her toy discovery. She waves at me and then goes right back to the toys.

Bailey looks at me—fuck, does she look at me. I can tell she is trying not to cry, and that shit hurts my fucking soul. She is so tiny; it fucking pisses me off that she has had such a hard time with everything. Her fucking ex doesn't deserve to be alive for the shit she has been dealt. "One more thing." I reach into my pocket and take out the keys to the SUV. It's mine, but I have a truck so it's rarely used. "Here are the keys to the SUV. Use it for whatever you need to do and so you have a way to get to work." I press the keys into her hand. "I know you don't want to take it, but think of it as a loan."

She presses her mouth closed, and I can tell she's planning to say no, and it's taking everything in her to refuse. She really needs a fucking vehicle.

"I know how you like to be independent."

She lets out a deep breath. "You're right. Thank you guys again, so much."

I tighten my hand on hers. "I am right across the yard. If you need anything, let me know." I wait for her nod, and then I leave them—but, fuck, I want to stay.

Bailey

I watch him walk down the stairs, and I press my back against the wall. I hear Gabby inside her new bedroom, laughing and having the time of her life.

I walk to my bedroom and sit on the edge of the bed, feeling so overwhelmed by everything that has happened. Right before I met Adeline, my ex threw the papers at me after he signed away his paternal rights. Even before he signed away his rights, he wouldn't even let her call him

Dad; she calls him by his first name. It crushed me that he would do that to her.

He is the dumbest person in the world. He is missing out on the best thing in the universe; she is an angel on this earth. She is beautiful, she is precious, and he will never know anything as perfect as she is. He missed her first laugh, her first time crawling, and her first steps. He missed everything.

I could not imagine not having my baby. She is my whole heart and soul. Without her I am not sure what kind of person I would be right now.

I am glad, in a way, that he has no claim on her. We can cut him out of our lives, and she will not have to deal with the confusion anymore. Not that she asks about him. This is a fresh start for us, a new beginning.

Bailey

The next morning, I am making a huge breakfast because I am going to invite Travis, to thank him for everything he has done for us.

Gabby is awake, sitting on the couch watching TV. She is wearing pajamas covered in flowers. Her long hair is still a mess from rolling in her sleep so much. I take out my phone and shoot Travis a text inviting him to breakfast. In seconds he says he's on his way. I laugh at his quick reply. Now that I got a great night's sleep for the first time in such a long time, I feel pretty amazing. I felt safe in my new home, and Travis being right next door probably played a part that.

There is a knock at the door, "Ravis!" Gabby yells as I place the last plate on the table. She opens the door, and he steps inside, smiling at her so beautifully. Travis looks at me, and I feel the air being ripped from my lungs.

Stop it, Bailey, you need to chill out. He is just a beautiful man. He smiles and my stomach flips. But he is so much more than a beautiful man, isn't he? He walks over to me, and I swear every single step is another pound of my heart.

"Good morning, Bailey."

"Good morning, Travis. Sit down and I will grab Gabby."

He touches my back as he sits down at the table.

"Come on, baby, it's time for breakfast," I tell her, and she takes off in a run. She sits down beside Travis, and I fix her plate for her. I sit down with Travis between us. She grabs her fork and starts digging into her food.

"Looks good, Bailey," Travis says. I smile at him and begin eating my own food. From the corner of my eye, I watch him. His tattoos and the way his muscles move with every motion is infatuating. The scruff on his face ties everything together. His blue eyes are the best part, piercing right down to my very soul. It's like he sees every single part of me with just a glance.

Travis breaks the silence and interrupts my gaping. "Gabby, there is a park right down the street, would you like to go?"

She claps her hands together. "Really? Momma, can we go?" She looks at me with those big eyes. I laugh. "Yes, baby." She screams loudly, bouncing in her seat. Travis laughs at her antics. Once she gets used to the people around her, you will see her very goofy self. "Best day ever," she gushes and goes back to smashing the food into her mouth. She is a bottomless pit.

"She's precious," Travis tells me, causing my poor pitiful heart to flutter. *He likes my daughter!* She *is* precious, an angel sent right from heaven.

Gabby is chattering away to Travis. I enjoy seeing her so open to talking to someone she just met yesterday. It's been worrying me that she has been sheltered, because it's really just me and her.

We finish our food. "You guys go get ready and I will clean up." Travis takes the plate from my hand and carries it to the sink. The way he moves, the way he carries himself, is different. His confidence is so sexy to me.

I turn away from him, following Gabby up the stairs. I think I just really need to get laid. I have not had sex since before Gabby was born, and I am pretty sure I am a born-again virgin, if that's even possible. Sex was not that enjoyable for me anyway, so I am not sure what I am missing. I just miss being with someone.

I walk into Gabby's room and grab some clothes for her to change into. She can do that part herself; all I have to do is fix her hair. "Make sure you brush your teeth before you put your clothes on." I kiss the top of her head, catching her small smile, and walk into my room to quickly get ready. I slip on a pair of jeans and a V-neck shirt, and I brush my long, wavy brown hair before adding some texturing spray. My daughter has been blessed with amazing ringlets from her dad—his only good quality, in my opinion—the rest of her is me. She is my mini-me. I've got to admit I am that mom who has outfits that match her daughter's.

I throw my hair into a bun because it's already hot outside. There's a little knock on the door, and Gabby walks into the room. She is holding her hairbrush and a tie. She climbs on the bed and turns her back to me, and I put her hair into a French braid to keep it out of her face.

"I will call and see what gymnastics classes they have around here." She is my little athlete. She is small, but she is amazing at gymnastics. I tie off her hair and let it go. She spins around, her eyes absolutely glowing. "Thank you, Mommy!" she screams, hopping up onto the bed, and she wraps me in a hug. I hug her back, breathing in her shampoo. My precious baby.

"You're more than welcome, baby." I kiss her cheek and help her off the bed. She takes my hand and pulls me out of the room. "RAVIS! Guess what!" she screams.

He walks around the corner, wiping his hands on a dish towel. "Yeah, sweetheart?"

She jumps up and down. "Mommy is going to sign me up for gymnastics!"

He laughs. "Your mom is the best." Travis winks at me. Fuck my life.

Travis

The sight of Gabby dragging her mom down the stairs, with absolute happiness pouring off her, is purely amazing. That shit needs to be protected in this world.

There is so much fucking horrible shit in this world that it's good for your soul to see something so innocent and carefree. Bailey is just a beautiful woman, and the way she carries herself lets me know that she has dealt with some shit in her life but she came out on top. That is fucking amazing. I know she had her daughter young, but she pushed through all of that.

I want to know more about her. I don't give a fuck if it's about her favorite nail polish. I just want to be around her and her daughter. Gabby is a mini version of her mother. "You guys ready?" I ask them.

Bailey is in the kitchen grabbing some snacks for Gabby. She stuffs everything in a fancy pink lunch box. I take the lunch box from her. Her eyes widen at seeing me holding this girly purse shit, but I don't give a fuck. She isn't going to carry shit in front of me.

"I like your purse, Ravis." Gabby giggles.

I throw the strap dramatically over my shoulder and wink down at her. "Looks good on me, doesn't it?"

Bailey throws her head back laughing, her eyes brightening beautifully. "You look really pretty," Bailey says.

Pretty, huh? I split the distance between us, and I bend down and whisper in her ear. "I don't think *pretty* is a word I would use to describe myself. You are the one who's pretty, Momma."

Her mouth falls open slightly; I tap her chin and she shuts it. I chuckle under my breath and walk to the front door, leaving her with her thoughts. It's going to be fucking amazing to get into her head, weaseling my way into her mind until she can't get me out.

As we're leaving, I take the keys from Bailey's hand and lock the door for her. I can feel her watching me, confused as to why I am here—but she will get a clue. I turn around to look at her, and she looks away.

Gabby is twirling around in circles behind her.

"Come on, baby." Bailey taps her shoulder and takes her hand to help her down the stairs.

I step in front of them, opening Bailey's car door for her; then I help Gabby into her car seat. As I buckle her in, I notice Bailey standing there watching us. "Get in, I got her." She looks hesitant, but I want to help her out. I know she is not fucking used to any kind of help, but that is going to change now that she is being welcomed into the club. I would not be surprised if Adeline comes over this evening to make sure she is doing okay.

I shut Gabby's door and get in on the driver's side. Bailey is still standing outside her open door, "You getting in, sweetheart?" I smirk at her stunned expression. Her face reddens but she gets in. I wait until she is buckled in; then I back out of the driveway.

Every single house on this street belongs to the MC; this is where most of the single members of the club stay. We have another property outside of town where we built our family homes; we all stick together. That is what family should do.

"Do you want to go to the park here, or do you want to go the bigger one inside the city?" I ask.

"Bigger one!!" Gabby screams from the back seat and I laugh. I press the button opening the gate, and we go into town. Bailey's eyes are glued to the window, taking in everything we pass. We arrive at a cluster of shopping centers. "This is your salon." I point to a big building.

"Oh wow, it's huge." She leans forward to get a better view. I smile at her awed expression; she is beautiful. I look in the rearview mirror to check on Gabby, and she waves at me.

A few minutes later, we pull up outside the park. "WOW!" Gabby says, bouncing in her seat.

"I think she is a bit excited," Bailey says and I help Gabby out of the seat. She runs to Bailey. "Mom, this is the biggest one we've been to yet." She jumps up and down clapping her hands together, her long hair swinging all around her.

Bailey smiles down at her daughter. Jesus, she is fucking beautiful. "Run ahead, baby, we will be right behind you." Gabby runs across the grass, as fast as her little legs can take her, to the playground and Bailey laughs. "I think I am really going to like it here." She looks at me, smiling with delight.

"I am glad you decided to come here. Everyone needs a fresh start," I tell her, and her smile falls. *You're fucking stupid, Travis. You just brought up shit she is probably trying to forget.*

We walk together to a bench in front of the playground. Bailey sets her bag on the ground in front of her, and I sit down next to her, our legs touching.

Bailey

My first thought is why must he sit so close? He is wearing a white T-shirt under his vest, his tattoos on full display. He is just sexy.

I do have a thing for bad boys. I have tried to date the homegrown good ole boys but, honestly, my heart doesn't go pitter patter, and it's like *can I go home now?* Travis, on the other hand? His leg is touching mine, and I am internally freaking out. His huge tattoo-covered hand is resting on his knee, which is very close to my leg.

"Look, Ravis!" Gabby screams and jumps on the balance beam.

He jumps up. "She's going to get hurt." He starts to walk in her direction, and she does a flip on the beam.

"She loves gymnastics," I inform him, and he lets out a breath and sits beside me. "I can see her being in the Olympics. That is her dream in life, and I want her to be able to achieve that." I can feel him staring at me intensely, and I bite my lip pretending not to notice. It's kind of hard to look him in the eye. Hell, it's hard to even look at such a beautiful man. He intimidates me with his confidence and the way he carries himself, which reflect the fact that he knows himself.

Do I know myself? I know that I lost myself when I became pregnant and was all alone in the world. I never had a chance to come to terms with what has happened with my life. My parents completely abandoned me; my mother threw me out of the house and never looked back because my pregnancy caused her friends to look down on her.

When I had my daughter, I saw a light at the end of the tunnel. I had been so alone in the world, but I had this beautiful, precious baby girl in my arms, and she needed me. That gave me hope. My daughter's name is Gabrielle LeAnn Mathis. She has my last name. He was not even there for her birth; the only time that he came around was to hold her over my head. He had money and lawyers, and I had absolutely nothing. I was terrified. I would lie awake at night, scared of what life would be without Gabby. Then he signed his rights over and I was free, and now here I am.

Travis interrupts my thoughts. "What has you thinking so hard?"

I laugh. "Oh, nothing."

"M-hm," his deep, beautiful voice murmurs. How is even that sexy?

I look at Gabby, and I know immediately something is not right. She is clutching her right side, above her hip. She stumbles to the edge of the playground and vomits.

I run over to her and hold her hair out of her face. "What is wrong, baby?"

She groans and continues holding onto her side.

Travis stands on her other side. "Does your side hurt?" He asks her.

She nods and ducks her head, and I can see tears falling down her face.

"Let's get her to the hospital, something is wrong," I tell him, and he picks her up off the ground. I grab our bag in front of the bench, and I reach inside Travis's pocket and unlock the SUV. I open the door for him, and he gently sets Gabby in her booster seat.

She holds onto her side, crying harder. I look at Travis in panic. "She usually tries to hold it in when she's hurting, so she must really be in pain," I whisper.

"Shh, we will be at the hospital soon," he tells her while buckling her in, and he shuts the door. When we're all in the car, Travis looks back at Gabby then at me. I can tell it's bothering him, and it's shattering my heart to hear her cries.

He takes out his phone and calls someone. "Myra, I have a patient for you. We will be there in about ten minutes." He listens for a moment. "She is claiming her right side is hurting her." He listens again and hangs up. "She is a pediatrician and wife of one of the guys in the neighboring MC." He speeds up going down the highway.

"Mommy, I am sick again."

I look around frantically for something for her to vomit in, and then I hear it and smell it. I reach inside my bag and grab some wipes. She is pale, very pale. My stomach is twisting at the sight of her so sick. She has never had anything more serious than a cold. "How long have you been feeling bad, angel?" I brush aside some hair that has come loose from her braid.

"A few days, Mommy, it came and went." I close my eyes. My baby is strong. I clean her off as much as possible. I will change her at the hospital. Luckily, I bring extra clothes for her everywhere I go. I stare at her the whole ride to the hospital.

"I hurt, Mommy!" Tears fall down her face. The truck pulls to a stop and Travis gets out before I even know we are there. I climb out and grab my bag. He lifts her out of her seat, and she lays her head against his chest with her eyes closed.

A woman is waiting for us at the entrance. She looks at Gabby. "We have a room ready for her." We follow her into the hospital and to a room, Travis sets Gabby down on the bed, and she buries her head in the pillow.

"Let me take a look at you, sweetheart. I'm Myra by the way." Myra looks at me . I take a step back, right into Travis. He presses his hand to the small of my back, and I look up at him—but his eyes are on my daughter. I can see he is concerned.

Myra has Gabby lying flat on her back, and she touches the side causing the pain. Gabby cries out and sits up in bed. I cover my mouth with my hand, stifling a scream.

"I need to do some blood work, but I do believe it may be her appendix."

She leaves and I take her place next to Gabby. "Want to change out of that dirty shirt, baby?" I smooth her hair out of her face. She nods her head, and I look at Travis. He walks to the other side of the room and pulls the curtain closed. I help her out of her shirt and reach in my bag for more wipes.

After cleaning her as well as possible, I slip the clean shirt over her head and settle her back in bed. I touch her forehead, and she feels hot. "She is dressed," I tell Travis, and he opens the curtain and walks to her other side. Her entire body is shivering. "She has a fever," I whisper, and he touches her forehead like this is the most natural thing in the world. "I wonder if there is a blanket in here?" I ask myself.

"I will go find one. I will be back in a moment."

I stare at his retreating back and look back at my daughter. Her eyes are closed and the sight of her just lying there, so pale, and not even knowing what is officially wrong with her is horrible.

Travis returns with a blanket and an extra pillow. He unfolds the blanket and covers her, tucking her in. Then he places the pillow beside her face, and she rolls over, curling around it. There is a small knock and I turn around to see a nurse with a case, letting me know she is here to draw blood.

"Sweetheart, she needs to take some blood." I rub Gabby's arm and she opens her eyes. I can see her fear. "It will be over in a second, and that'll be it."

The nurse goes to her other side and takes her arm. Gabby looks me dead in the eyes without flinching as her arm is dabbed with the alcohol wipe.

Travis sits in a chair beside me, and I look away while Gabby is stuck with the needle. Her eyes fill with tears once again, her bottom lip trembling. This is killing my soul.

Travis reaches forward and catches her tear. "You are brave, sweetheart," he whispers, and she manages a small smile. I smile at her, and she closes her eyes again. She is exhausted.

How did I not know she was sick? She has slept so much in the past couple of days, but I thought she was tired from the plane ride and the move. I should have known she did not feel well. What kind of mother am I?

When the nurse leaves, I run my fingers along the top of Gabby's head. "Sleep, baby, I am right here."

She nods her little head, and with my free hand I bring the blanket up to her neck. A hand touches me, and I peek around and see Travis stroking my back.

"Thank you for bringing me here and having Myra get her in so quickly," I whisper, so it doesn't disturb her.

"It was nothing, Momma, I just want her to feel better." Why do I find that so attractive? His calling me *Momma*? But I think he could call me a potato and I would like it.

We sit and wait, and it seems like forever before Myra comes back. "It seems that her appendix is extremely close to rupturing, immediate surgery is needed."

My heart sinks and shatters. I knew Gabby was sick, but an operation? I nod at Myra, but I cannot give her my words because they seem lost. "I will get everything set in motion," Myra informs me, and I nod again. My mouth is dry, and my throat feels like it's closing together.

A Couple of Hours Later

As they push my daughter away in her bed, I cover my mouth. It takes everything in me not run after her to tear her away.

"Bailey," Travis says and, when I look at him, tears that have been trying to fall since the moment I found out Gabby needed surgery pour out. His face softens in a way that I have not seen before, his hand wraps around the back of my neck, and my face rests on the center of his chest. I fist his shirt, and he settles one hand on the back of my head and the other on my back. "She will be fine," he whispers to me, lips pressing against the top of my head. I close my eyes and, for the first time in years, I allow myself to not be strong, to let someone take the burden off of me. I have not been held or comforted in so long that it seems foreign, but I need this. His smell wraps around me like a protective bubble. He sits down with me in a room without a bed.

"She has never been sick like this before. She's my baby and it kills me to see her go through things like that."

"I know, sweetheart, but she will be better before you know it." He settles back into his seat and takes me with him. I close my eyes and dry my tears. The time for being weak is over, but I will allow myself to continue to be in his arms. Who would dare leave?

Travis

What a fucking day, I knew the moment I saw Gabby bent over holding her side that something was wrong. The sight of her pale face and then her getting sick? I could feel it right to my fucking core.

Bailey is curled into my chest, asleep. She is mentally drained. I have seen a lot of amazing mothers, but I have never seen anyone who loves her daughter as much as Bailey loves Gabby. It gives me such great pleasure that she is letting me comfort her. I know that she has been alone for so long, but I want her to know that is not the case anymore.

A nurse pops her head into the room. "I am here to take you to the waiting room, to wait for her to get out."

"Sweetheart, wake up."

Bailey jumps away, her hair a mess. "Is she out?"

"No, sweetheart, we are being taking to the waiting room." I instinctively smooth her hair out of her face. She gets out of her chair, yawning. I take out my phone and shoot a text to Wilder, asking him if he can bring me some food, clothes, and other things we'll need for a few days. I am not leaving her alone. Never again.

Bailey

She is out of surgery and it's now night time; she is back in her room resting. She is pretty doped up on medication but, thankfully, she is going to be fine.

The weight of the world was lifted off my shoulders the moment they told me that they had caught it just in time and she is going to be perfectly okay. For the first time that day, I could finally breathe. I thought Travis would leave once the doctors said she would be alright, but he's asleep sitting up in a chair. He was right by my side the whole time. I wasn't alone. It's such a strange feeling.

I see an extra blanket at the foot of her bed. I stand up, unfold it, and gently cover him up. His eyes are open, staring at me. A warm, fuzzy feeling hits me right in the pit of the stomach. "Thank you, Travis," I whisper, smiling at him, and I turn away. I do not want him to see what I am really feeling right now, because I am not sure of that myself.

He had his friend brings us blankets, food, and clothes, along with toiletries to make sure we are comfortable. He thought of everything. What he is doing right now means more to me that anything else in this world: just being here. I grab my pillow and blanket and curl up the best I can in my small chair. Then I close my eyes, hopefully to a wake up to a better day.

three

Travis

I wake up to a finger poking me in the face, and I open my eyes and see Gabby staring at me. "How are you feeling?" I touch her arm.

"My tummy hurts and I am hungry," she whispers. I look over at Bailey and see she is sound asleep.

"I will go get a nurse for you, okay?" Gabby nods her head, and her body is shaking again. I touch her forehead. She is cool—it must be the room; hospitals are really cold. I cover her up with my blanket; then I walk to the nurses' station. I inform them of what is happening, and a nurse grabs a breakfast tray. I take it from her. "Please be as quiet as possible. Her mother is exhausted." She nods and we quietly walk back into the room.

The nurse goes over to Gabby's IV and puts in some pain medication. "That should feel better soon now. Try to eat as much as you can."

I place the tray on the table. "Do you need me to feed you?"

She nods and I help her sit up so she can eat easily. "Thank you, Ravis."

I smile at her. "Anything for you, sweet girl." I touch the side of her face.

Bailey

I wake up to the most beautiful sound in the world, the sound of my baby's giggles, and then the most incredible sight. Travis is feeding my daughter breakfast; I think this the most surprising thing yet. His hair is all messed up on top, and his clothes are rumpled from his sleep. "Another?" he asks her softly. She nods, and he gives her another bite of eggs. "Your belly feel better?"

"The medicine made it feel better." She hesitantly reaches down to touch her side, and Travis stops her.

"Don't touch it, honey." I close my eyes when I notice Travis looking at me, and I don't want this moment to end. So I pretend.

"Ravis, can you fix my hair?" Gabby asks and I try to hold in my laughter.

"I can try." I can hear him walking into the bathroom. I crack my eyes open, and Gabby is staring right at me, smiling. I am totally busted.

"Go back to sleep, Momma," she whispers and I close my eyes, trying to hide my smile, just as Travis walks back out. I peek just a little bit.

"I have no clue what I am doing, you just want me to brush it?" Travis asks.

"Braid it too, please."

His eyes widen, and I cover my mouth with my blanket. He helps her move to where he can reach her hair easily. He puts the brush at the crown of her head then brings it down until it snags on a tangle. She winces.

"I'm sorry, I am not good at this shit." Gabby giggles at his cuss words. "Fuck, your mom is going to kill me," he grumbles and she laughs because he did it again. "She is going to kill me for sure now," he says a little louder than a grumble and I laugh this time, not able to help myself.

He looks over at me accusingly. "You were awake the whole time, weren't you?"

I sit up and wink and he smirks at me. I walk over and take the hairbrush from him. "Thank you, Travis." He smiles at me beautifully. It should be a crime for a man to look this good in the mornings. I probably look like shit, honestly.

He touches my back, getting my attention. "Want me to go downstairs and get us some breakfast?"

"You don't..." I stop at the look on his face and roll my eyes. "That will be great. Thank you, Travis."

He smiles that flipping smile and leaves the room just like that.

"He's funny, Mommy."

"He is…and very nice." I continue brushing her hair

"Can we go home today?" she asks, and I stop midstroke. "I am not sure. It's up to your doctor, baby."

"Maybe if we are really nice he will say yes. Or if I do the look that gets you to say yes for toys."

I laugh, patting her on the back. "You just told on yourself, Gabby."

She covers her mouth with her hand. "Uh oh."

"Uh oh…yes, little girl."

She laughs. She knows she isn't in trouble, because I have known of this look since she was old enough to make it. I put her hair in a loose French braid to keep it out of her face. She doesn't need to come back to have the stitches taken out, thank goodness. It's a small incision, but it was scary just the same. The thought of something going wrong or her not waking up was deep in my mind.

Later, Travis shows up with two bags. He hands me one and I smile.

"Thank you, Travis, this means so much." I don't want to seem ungrateful.

He doesn't say anything for a few beats; he just stares at me, his eyes locked on mine. "No thanks are needed." He cups his hand around the back of my neck.

Gabby is lying back in bed, her eyes drifting closed, watching cartoons.

"Tired, baby?" She nods. I reach over, but Travis beats me to it and brings the blanket up to her chin. He confuses me. I am not used to seeing a guy having such a nurturing side. My father doesn't; I don't even think he ever hugged me. My mother wasn't either. I had a nanny until I was old enough to take care of myself.

One of the most devastating things that happened to me as a kid was when my nanny was let go. She was the only mother figure I'd ever had. I think that is why I let so much go when I was dating Gabby's father. I wanted to be loved so much, because I'd never had that growing up.

I am glad all of that is over. I am in a new place with new people, and these people are like saints or something.

I finish my food, stuff all of my empty wrappers in the garbage, and walk over to get Travis's before he can do it himself. The death glare that I just got should be enough to scare me, but that is one thing I am not: scared. Under the mean-looking exterior, he is a big softy. Well, to me and Gabby, that is. I know he is a dangerous man, but I see the side that stayed with me in the hospital, comforted me, and tried to fix my daughter's hair. I see how comfortable Gabby is with him. She is usually shy around everyone but me. But she's never been that way around him. Not once.

"I will stay with her, go do what you need to do," he tells me. I hesitate, looking at Gabby, even though I have to fill out some paperwork—I had to get a lot of stuff faxed over from Hawaii.

Travis

The moment Bailey leaves, Gabby opens her eyes and looks at me. I lean over the bed railing. "You need something?"

She shakes her head, studying me. "Do you want to be my momma's boyfriend?" That is not what I expected her to say.

"I would love to be your momma's boyfriend. We just have to get her to like the idea." I wink at her.

She smiles, hitting me right in the fucking chest. "I think she already likes you." She whispers the last part, looking at the door.

"Teamwork?" I put my fist out for her to bump. She bumps her tiny fist against mine, and I laugh. She is adorable.

"I'm going to sleep now." She yawns, covering her mouth. "Will you hold my hand, Ravis, until Momma gets back?" Last night, she fell asleep holding Bailey's hand; she was scared to be in the hospital.

"Sure, baby." I put down the railing, and her tiny hand completely disappears in mine. The top of her head barely reaches my hip. With every flutter of her eyes closing, a bit of my heart falls away. It hits me all at once. My brothers have been telling me all along I would know. I know this little girl is supposed to be mine; she is supposed to be my daughter. Don't ask me how I know this, but when I look at her it's like my heart reclaims a piece I never knew was missing.

I pull the blanket up under her chin and push her bangs out of her face. Freckles brush the tops of her nose and cheeks. "Sleep, little princess," I whisper as her eyes finally close. She squeezes my hand. It's like she knows.

#

Bailey

A Week Later

Gabby and I are sitting on the couch watching TV. She is doing a lot better; she's almost back to herself.

There's a small knock at the door before Travis steps inside the house. One part of me thought once we were home he would go back to his own schedule. That is not the case. He stays with us all day long until bedtime, and he is back first thing in the morning.

The thing is, I want him around. I want him to be with us; it's comforting. He makes me feel safe, and Gabby really likes him. They are like two peas in a pod.

"Hey, Ravis," Gabby calls and he smiles at her so blindingly. She scoots over and leaves him a spot between us. He sits a little closer to me than her and looks at me like he's the cat catching the mouse.

"What?" I ask.

"Tonight you and I are going out," he says in a matter-of-fact way.

"Yeah? What for?"

"Baby, I am taking you out on a date. Wilder and Joslyn are coming over to watch Gabby for us."

What? He is really asking me out on a date? My mouth opens and closes; I don't know what to say. It's been so long. Of course I like him. I have liked him since the moment I met him. He is absolutely gorgeous, and he's so kind to me and my daughter. Why wouldn't I go? I study his face for a few moments before I nod. "Yeah, I will go." I say softly.

"YAY!" Gabby dances a little on her seat on the couch. I eye her. Aha! I *thought* she was being sneaky, always making sure we were sitting together.

"You guys were in on this, weren't you?" I smile.

"Of course we were, Momma," Gabby sings and I laugh loudly. At least I don't have to worry about whether Gabby likes him. I grab my throw blanket, which has fallen to the floor, and pull it back over my legs. I unpause the movie and curl into the arm of the chair.

We have been lazy for the last week. I wanted Gabby to heal and relax. So we have been doing everything possible to keep her entertained.

Adeline has been by every single day to check in on us; that woman is such a beautiful soul. Every time she is around, I feel that I'm surrounded by motherly love. Something I wish my own mother had given me, but she must have missed that gene. I just can't fathom it. Gabby is everything to me, and the idea of not being an involved parent is crazy. She is my life.

I love being a mother more than anything. I want to have least one or two more kids someday. I think it's a dream most women have: a family—that white fence with two point five kids.

"Wear something casual," Travis says. "You will be on the back of my bike."

I have never been on a motorcycle; what if I fall off? What do I say? "Okay."

He gives me that way-too-beautiful smile once again, and I think I would agree to anything. I lean against the arm of the chair. When I start to pull my blanket up, Travis does it for me. I am in so much trouble.

His hand gets closer and closer to my face, and his fingertips touch my cheek before drifting into my hair. I close my eyes and let out a shaky breath, and goose bumps break out across my arms. The sensation of him stroking my hair is out of this world. I'm in more trouble than I thought I was; I think I am totally screwed.

Around five o'clock, I walked upstairs to start getting ready for my date, and now it's ten till seven.

I am wearing a tight pair of skinny jeans with holes scattered throughout both legs. I am wearing a pair of booties, and the bottoms of my jeans are rolled up just a tad. My burgundy cold-shoulder top brings out my dark brown hair, which is in loose waves around my face, and my green eyes. My makeup is on point; the perks of being a makeup artist are paying off.

Travis has not seen me this way. He has seen the scatterbrained mom who's so busy the last thing on her mind is getting dressed up. I let out a deep breath, eyes closed, as I collect myself before going downstairs.

Travis's cousin Wilder and his wife, Joslyn, are on the couch with Gabby. Gabby notices me first. "Wow, you're pretty, Momma."

I smile and walk over to her. "Thank you, angel." I press my lips to the top of her head. "It's nice to meet you guys," I tell Wilder and Joslyn.

"It's nice to meet you too." Joslyn touches my forearm, and I nod at Wilder. He does look like Travis; I can see it in his hair color and facial features.

My front door opens, and Travis steps inside the house looking way too amazing. He is wearing a pair of jeans, biker boots, and a black T-shirt with his leather vest resting on top. His hair is swept to the side slightly with gel, and his tattoos are on display. He is absolutely beautiful, like the walk-into-the-wall-because-I'm-staring-so-hard kind of beautiful. He is even more beautiful on the inside; his heart is kind. That is something I have not encountered often. I need this energy change; it's like my body and soul just feel lighter. Freer.

Travis leans against the doorframe, arms across his chest. I bite the inside of my lip watching his eyes moving up and down my body. I can feel my heart beating, and my stomach is doing twists and turns. I clear my throat, and he finally smiles and splits the distance between us.

"Aren't you beautiful, Bailey," he whispers, pushing my hair over my shoulder. My face is hot with embarrassment. I can feel Gabby's, Wilder's, and Joslyn's eyes on us. Travis hasn't even looked at them from the moment he walked into the house. "Ready to go?" he asks. He touches my chin and I nod.

Someone clears their throat, and Travis turns around to face Wilder, who has a smirk on his face. "Nice of you to finally notice us," Wilder says and Gabby laughs.

"Yeah, Ravis."

I laugh. I love it when she throws out her sass. She is such a little diva.

"Have fun, Momma." She smiles and I touch the side of her face.

"I will, baby. Be good for them, okay?"

"I will." She nods her little head, acting way older than her age. She is so cute I can't stand it sometimes.

"She will be fine," Joslyn reassures me.

"Thank you for watching her, both of you." I look at her and Wilder, and Wilder nods.

"Come on, Momma." Travis intertwines our fingers and leads me out of the house. I peek back at Gabby one last time. She is sitting on the floor with Joslyn, who is playing dolls with her. She will be fine. I'm not sure if *I* will be.

The door shuts behind us, and I follow Travis down the steps to his bike, which is parked in front. He swings his leg over the bike and sits down, and I stand next to him, clueless about what I am to do.

He points his finger down. "Put your leg here, and then swing your other leg over and sit down. I will help you." He reaches out and I place my hand in his, and I throw my leg over the seat. I let his hand go, and his hands wrap around my calves. "Oh, here." He reaches into the saddle bag and hands me a leather jacket and a helmet.

I slip on the jacket and put on the helmet, snapping the buckle. "Good?" I ask and he turns around to check me over.

He smiles. "Perfect, Momma." Oh bless my heart, his deep voice goes straight down to my valuable parts. They have been singing since the moment I met him, but I have been ignoring it because I do need to get laid but I can't—like—jump his bones, no matter how much I want to. "Wrap your arms around my waist."

I lean forward and do as he asks; then the bike comes alive with a roar. He tilts his head back. "Ready?"

"Yeah."

Then we are off, my hair flying out behind me. I rest my chin on his shoulder, kind of scared but, at the same time, it is freeing. When we pull into traffic, it's kind of scary; I know that a lot of people don't watch for

motorcycles. When we stop at a red light, I readjust myself in my seat to get more comfortable and loosen my death grip on him. A car pulls to a stop next to us; it is full of men staring at me. I turn away, ignoring them.

"Hey, baby."

Travis

"Hey baby." That shit ran right through me. I look over at the fuckers, but they are staring at Bailey's ass.

I press my hand against her side to shield her ass. I do not fucking like disrespect, especially not toward Bailey. "Hey fucker, what are you doing?" I look the driver straight in the fucking eye and, with my free hand, I take out my gun and point it in their direction. Their eyes widen; then the light turns green and they look straight ahead and drive off. I laugh at their luck and put my gun back. Bailey is laughing her ass off. It makes me feel fucking good to know that she is okay with what I did. I don't tolerate shit like that, especially right in front of my face.

She moves closer to me, tucking herself against me. I grin. I love the feeling of her against my back. The sight of her resting behind me. She is fucking gorgeous, and she is fucking mine—she just doesn't know that shit yet. This is just the first step, until it clicks in her brain that I am not going anywhere. Every single day I notice the surprise on her face when I walk through her front door. If it were up to me, I would never leave at night. I would stay on the fucking couch or in her bed, but I know better than to suggest the latter.

At least I have Gabby on my side. She is super sly about it. She always makes sure that her mother and I end up sitting together.

I pull up in front of a steakhouse and park in a section in front that's reserved for the MC. We own this place. The Devil Souls MC owns all of the restaurants in Raleigh, Texas, and we own almost everything here, aside from the chain stores, which have become very successful in small towns. We are doing very well for ourselves.

Bailey holds my shoulder as she throws her leg over the bike, and she takes off her helmet and shakes her head, letting her hair fall around her. Fuck me.

She stops and looks at me, and I am completely staring at her. "What is it?" Her mouth is pressed into a little pout. So fucking beautiful. It's a shame that she doesn't even know it.

"You're fucking gorgeous," I tell her, and she blushes right down to her chest. I laugh and touch her warm cheek. She pushes my hand away, looking away from me, pretending that I don't affect her. She can pretend all she fucking wants to, but I do.

That doesn't mean that I am going to play along. Little by little I will break her down and get her to see me. "Come on, Momma, let's get you fed before the real fun starts." I put my hand on the small of her back, leading her inside the steakhouse.

"What do you mean?"

I wink. I am going to take her to an MC bar. We own the bar, and I know some of the brothers are going to be there tonight. I want her to let loose and have fun, something I know she has not done in a very long time.

Bailey

Have some fun? What did he mean by that? He is just giving me that sly little smile.

As he holds the door open for me and I step inside, I notice him staring at my ass. *Caught you.* I raise my eyebrows at him, and he grins even wider. I can tell that he is not fazed at all, which is quite frustrating, considering.

We grab a seat toward the back, and I sit down in a booth and scoot to the middle. I expect him to sit across from me, but he parks his butt in the seat next to me. "Uhh, what are you doing?" My insides are jumping with him being so close. I am nervous, and who can blame me? Look at him. If God could make the perfect creation, then this is it.

"Sitting by the beautifulest woman in this restaurant?" He pushes my hair over my shoulder. Oh my word, this man.

"Thank you, Travis, you're sweet." I tell him, and he turns his face away.

"I'm not fucking sweet."

I laugh.

"Yes you are, you're a big softy."

He shakes his head. "Do not start this shit, Momma. I'm a badass."

I laugh louder and open my menu. "Keep telling yourself that, Travis." I nudge his side with my elbow. He chuckles, grabbing my hand and pulling it into his lap so we can twine our fingers together, calm and unfazed. He is just holding my hand, and I am freaking out. My skin is tingling from that light touch, and I can feel his eyes on me. "What are you getting?" I ask, to break the silence that is wrecking my soul.

"Steak."

I roll my eyes and continue to look at my menu. I look at the cheapest thing on the menu, and it's soup.

"Do not fucking dare get the cheapest thing on the menu," he sasses me and I look at him full on, my mouth open in disbelief.

"Maybe I just want soup?"

"Momma, you skipped over everything else on the menu." He arches an eyebrow at me, daring me to argue. Grrr.

"Well, I can't afford much."

He jolts like he is shocked. "Why the fuck does that matter? You aren't buying anything, ever, in my presence."

I suck in my lips. My ex never bought me anything when we were out. I look at the menu then at him, "I didn't want to assume. I usually buy my own meal," I confess to him, and I regret it the moment I do. I don't want anyone to know of the horrible times I went through. I never even knew what I was going through until I'd been on my own for a while. I realized my life had not been normal. Now it is even more clear to me. I've seen the way people here treat each other, and it's been another huge wake-up call to me.

He rests his elbow on the table and looks at me. I swallow hard at his full attention. "What the fuck do you mean?" he asks.

I close my eyes for a few seconds. I just ruined it all. He lets go of my hand. Yeah, I ruined it. A hand touches my jaw. "Sweetheart?" I look at him again, and I might as well continue digging my own grave. No guy wants someone with baggage. "Nothing, I am not used to someone buying my dinner." I throw it out there and laugh it off. I am overthinking. I know this, but anxiety is real and a bitch.

He stares at the table for a few seconds, and his neck reddens. "You mean to tell me Gabby's father never even bought your meal?" His tone has changed and it's... deadly.

I clear my throat. "No, he never did anything." Oh my god, I just let out more than I should have.

"He is a worthless piece of shit is what he is," Travis says. I look down at the menu, saddened—because it's absolutely true. He touches my chin, tilting my face up. His face is soft. "He did not deserve you or your precious baby." My eyes fill with tears at his beautiful, kind words. He puts his hand on the back of my neck, and I bury my face in his chest, breathing in his scent: just Travis.

"I bet this is not what you expected on this date." I laugh and wipe away a tear. I guess he is okay with it.

"This is better than I expected, now pick yourself out a damn steak." He pats the side of my ass, and I laugh louder. I sit up straighter, feeling better, and I smile at him. I think sometimes I just need to let someone see what I have been through. I never had anyone to talk to about anything, so this is a load off of me.

But I'm still terrified of seeming needy around Travis. I have a huge fear of people leaving my life. It all started when my mother abandoned me when I was pregnant; then all of my friends left and Gabby's father left. Everyone just left. I was all alone, a teenager with a baby struggling to survive. I lived off of Ramen noodles for a whole year, and I can't remember the last time I had steak.

I look at my menu again, perusing the steak dinners. "You sure?" I ask.

"Momma, get whatever the fuck you want." He smirks, letting me know he is playing. I think he may kill me.

The waitress comes by a second later and takes our order. Travis orders an appetizer; I haven't eaten like this in a long time. I know this wouldn't seem like a big deal to a lot of people, but to me this is huge. I haven't had a really good meal in a long time. Gabby got the best food—she is my angel—and whatever was left over was for me. I even went for three to four days without eating so Gabby had a roof over her head and food in her belly. I do not regret a single second; I would do it all over again in a heartbeat. I am proud of the fact that Gabby has never ever been deprived of anything. She is the most important thing in my life.

The appetizer comes and we both dig in; I make sure there's nothing left. I am not wasting a thing. I do this again with my salad. I can feel him looking at me, but I ignore it--he does it a lot. "I don't think you know how beautiful you are, Bailey."

I smile at him; he is so sweet. "Thank you, Travis." I lean my head on his shoulder for a second, and he kisses the top of my head. Did that just happen? That was so cute.

Our food comes, and my mouth waters at the sight and smell of the steak and mashed potatoes. "Thank you, Travis, for the food."

"How long did you go?" he asks. He hasn't even touched his food yet.

"What do you mean?"

He licks his lips. Oh, he shouldn't do that with me around. He is asking to be kissed. He pushes my hair over my shoulder so casually it's like he doesn't even notice himself doing small affectionate things. "How long did you go without eating?"

My mouth falls open. How in the world did he know this? I sure never told anyone; can he read minds? "Travis, what?" I don't know what to say or how to act.

He looks away, his head hanging. "I hope the fuck I am wrong, the way you made sure nothing was wasted. And a bunch of other stuff I have noticed." How embarrassing is this? "I need to know, so I know how bad

I need to beat that motherfucker." He grins through clenched teeth. My heart is beating so hard I can feel it in my throat, and my hands are shaking.

"I have never been longer than three or four days. This happened every month when I didn't have clients. Gabby never, ever went without. She always had everything she needed," I whisper. I am so embarrassed.

He looks wrecked. "Momma, I am so fucking sorry. You're such an amazing fucking mother. I am in awe of you," he whispers. He leans over and kisses the top of my head, letting his lips rest against my hair for a few beats. My eyes close instinctively. That was the nicest thing anyone has ever said to me, and it touched my soul. All of my nervousness has gone away in a split second.

"Don't be sorry. Stuff happens, but it doesn't have to affect the now," I say. It's something I need to tell myself more often. Maybe saying it out loud to someone else will make it sink in?

"Fucking beautiful." He stares at me and shakes his head in disbelief. I am glad someone's speechless besides me. I touch my forehead to his shoulder for a second, showing him my gratitude. I am not great with words. I don't know what to say, but I also tend to overthink everything. I sure never expected our date to turn out the way it has so far—one surprise after another keeps hitting me. I don't regret it though. I am glad that he did not freak out when I revealed what little I did; I no longer feel like I'm walking on eggshells.

We finish up our food, and I eye the check when it comes. I am itching to just take it and run. Travis rolls his eyes like I am being cute, but when you're so used to being independent, it's kind of hard to let others take the lead.

"Ready to party?" He takes my hand, pulling me gently out of the booth. I laugh softly. "As ready as I will ever be."

Travis

I never expected to find out she was fucking starving, that she went days without eating just to make sure Gabby had everything she needed.

She is such a beautiful fucking woman—way too good for me, but I am a selfish bastard. And I know she will never, ever have to suffer again. Never again.

We are driving across town to a bar, where she will meet some of my brothers. This is my way of claiming her, letting others know she is mine. She is fucking mine. The moment she looked at me with those big beautiful eyes filled with tears, filled with fucking pain. The fear of me running away. That shit hit me right in the fucking core and hurt me; no one should have to suffer that way.

It pisses me off that every single person in her life has shit on her. They should have protected her and made sure nothing like that ever happened to her. They did shit. Her parents and especially the father of Gabby—that man needs to fucking die. I am pissed off at him for being a piece of shit. He crossed the fucking line when he allowed her to do without; he did absolutely nothing. I wanted to leave that fucking restaurant and track his ass down.

Someday—and it will happen soon—I want him to fucking suffer. I will bring him back to the club, and I will let him starve to fucking death just to see what she felt. I want him to feel every ounce of pain she has dealt with. They will all pay; that is for certain. Even her worthless fucking parents. They will know what she has gone through; that's for sure. Nobody—and I repeat *nobody*—fucks with Bailey.

It amazes me she is the way she is after everything that has happened to her; she still has that sweet innocence about her. I am going to protect and cherish that and her beautiful baby, Gabby. It will be my mission to make sure all of this happens—wait, no. It *will* happen.

five

Bailey

He holds the door open for me as I step inside the biker bar. This is the first bar I have ever been in, honestly. I was way too busy being a mom, and the thought never even crossed my mind—now here I am. I've never even drunk alcohol. I am a bit pathetic, honestly. What twenty-two-year-old hasn't indulged in a beer or been to a nightclub?

Travis puts his hand on the small of my back. I look around the room and I see a bunch of men and very few women. The women are all on the dance floor, half naked and having the time of their lives.

"Over here are my brothers," he says in my ear, and he leads me across the room. I can feel eyes on us from people all around us, which I ignore. "Hey, guys." He lets go of me for a second as he greets his brothers, doing that handshake hug thing all men seemed to have mastered from birth. I smile at all of them, and Travis looks at me and then back at the guys. "This is Bailey."

They nod and I try not laugh, because they all nod at the same exact time and it's such a badass thing to do. "Momma, this is our president, Lane." He points to the guy who is closest to me, and I reach out.

"It's nice to meet you." I smile at him. I want to make sure I give a good impression.

He points to the guy next to Lane. "This is Tristan."

I shake his hand. "Nice to meet you too." He laughs and looks at Travis, who is staring at me, smiling ear-to-ear. "The last one is Tristan's dad, Walker. My eyes widen slightly as I look at that silver fox of a man. He is beautiful—not as beautiful as my Travis, of course.

"Nice to meet you, little darlin'. My daughter is right around your age," he says, crushing any dream I ever had of dating an older man.

"You met Joslyn," Travis tells me.

"Ahh yes, she is a sweetheart," I tell Walker. I can see the resemblance now.

Walker touches Tristan's shoulder. "This is my son." Woah, the genes are strong in this family; that's for sure.

The door opens and Adeline comes in with a bunch more MC guys. She comes straight to me and pulls me into one of her motherly hugs. "How are you doing, sweetheart? How is Gabby?" She is talking a million miles an hour.

I laugh. "We are both good."

She smiles and smooths down the back of my hair with such motherly affection. I wish my mother were like her. I think of this almost daily—how different would my life have been?

"What do you want to drink?" Travis says in my ear, making me jump because I was lost in my thoughts. His breath on my face causes goosebumps to go straight down my spine. *Jeez, chill out, Bailey.*

"I really don't know, I never drank before." I shrug, feeling kind of self-conscious about the whole ordeal.

"That's alright, babe. I will grab you some fruity shit and then a beer. You can try both." He fixes my hair on my shoulder and walks away, leaving me speechless. I think I need to stop being in my head so much. I expect one thing, and he does the exact opposite.

That leaves me with Adeline and all of the guys. I can feel their eyes on me. I smile, and Adeline rubs my back. I guess she can tell I am nervous. "You having fun?" she asks, and I tear my eyes away from the guys and turn my attention to her.

"Yes, a lot of fun. Travis is just amazing." He really is the greatest guy I have ever met.

"He is a sweet boy. Just a heads-up, he is a major baby when he's sick though," she whispers and I laugh loudly. That's hilarious. A lot of men do tend to be horrible patients.

"Thanks for the heads-up." I laugh again at the thought of Travis lying in bed, a blanket tucked under his neck, pouting.

"Here, Momma." Travis is beside me, handing me a blue drink. "Try this."

"Thank you." I put the small cup up to my lips and take a sip. "Yum, this tastes like a pixie stick." I tilt the cup all the way back and finish it.

He laughs. "Here is a beer." I take it from him and take a drink. I cringe. "Yeah, I don't like this." I guess it's just an acquired taste.

"I will finish it for you, want another one of the drinks you like?"

I hesitate because, honestly, I don't want him to have to buy me anything else. His eyes narrow, and I bite the inside of my lip. "Thank you, Travis," I finally say, and he winks before walking back to the bar area. Adeline sighs, and she has a dreamy look in her eye.

"You okay?" I ask her.

"Travis is such a sweetheart."

I watch as he orders my drink, leaning against the bar. "Yeah, he really is." I don't take my eyes off him; just the way he moves is infatuating. I think I need to change. I need to get out of my head. What if I don't try with Travis? I would truly regret it. He has done nothing but prove himself to me and Gabby. I would be a fool to not just let go of all of the stupid stuff in my past and move forward. That is what I want to do, no more overthinking every detail. So what if it doesn't work out? In the end I will be perfectly fine. And what if it does?

He comes back with two more drinks. He hands me one and sets the other on the table in front of us. "Thank you." I smile and press myself against his side. This is outside of the norm for me. But I am doing what I have wanted to do since the very moment I met him.

He presses his hand against my back, rubbing gently. I feel him moving closer, and his lips touch my ear. "You okay, Momma?"

"More than okay. I have come to realize some things."

The expression on his face changes from confusion to pure happiness. He pulls me toward him so my back is lying against his chest. "You know how fucking happy you just made me? I needed and wanted you to see me from the very fucking second I met you," he whispers softly enough for only us to hear.

"I needed to wrap my head around it all. I needed to wrap my head around you." I lay my head against his chest. I can't believe I am really going to try and do this. I am going to try and have a relationship with this man, something that I never thought I would do again. He is different. I am different. This is just different. I need to stop comparing everything to the way things used to be.

"Fucking about time, Momma." His words send shivers down my back, and he bends down, kissing my forehead. I think that is the sweetest thing he's ever done. I smile and my cheeks are warm, not with embarrassment but with happiness. I turn around in his arms so that I'm facing him, shutting out everyone else in the room, giving us privacy.

I push my hair over my shoulder and take another sip of my drink. It's so good it might be dangerous, but I want to get at least slightly drunk.

Travis

When I came back with her drinks, I noticed a change in her instantly. She was more relaxed and, for a fucking split second, I was afraid she was done with me. Then she moved closer, until she was against my side, and I fucking knew she saw me.

I had wanted her to see the real me from the moment I met her. She has been so fucking hurt that she let that overshadow everything. I did everything in my power to wiggle my way into her life, but I didn't realize the full extent of the pain she'd suffered.

Now she's made me the happiest guy in the world. She is giving me the chance to show her that things can be different. She is giving me the chance to be the other half of her heart, which she has wrapped up so fucking tight. I am getting the chance to be a part of Gabby's life. She has let me in a little bit, but I am going to take that little bit and bury myself so fucking deep. She could do so much better than someone like me, but no one else would care for her the way I will. She is Bailey.

Bailey

It's getting later and the room is filled to the brim with people, dancing and grinding all over the place. The club is full of bikers. Most of them are not Grim Sinners; they're from surrounding small towns.

I rest my head on Travis's shoulder; the alcohol is taking effect. Someone starts laughing and I join.

"Someone's feeling a bit tipsy." Travis holds me more tightly against his side.

"Damn, you feel nice."

"Thank you." He chuckles.

My eyes snap open. Did I just say that aloud? "Did I just…" I ask.

"It's okay, Momma." He laughs under his breath again, and I smack him lightly on the chest and tear myself away. "I am going to the bathroom."

Adeline sets her beer down on the table. "I will go with you." We walk inside the bathroom, and I take a stall while Adeline stands in front of the mirrors, waiting for me.

I hear the door open and a bunch of women laughing. "Well, if it isn't a Grim Sinner bitch." What the hell? Adeline is wearing her cut, like all the women who are with their men. It's a sign of being under their protection, and it's sort of like marriage to them, or so I have been told. I hurry and pull my pants up and push open the stall. Adeline is in the corner surrounded by three women.

"I am so fucking sick of women like you thinking you're the shit," the woman on the right hisses in Adeline's face, "but you are not, and our guys are going to fucking show your guys who are the real badasses. Not some pussy wearing a cut."

Oh hell no. Adeline is the sweetest woman; I will not stand back and let them fucking do this to her. Did I ever mention I have a bit of a temper?

I grab my hair tie off my wrist and bundle my hair up on top of my head in a bun. I clear my throat, and they all turn to look at me. "Why don't you leave her alone and pick on me?" I smile at them, watching with glee as they look me up and down.

"What are you going to do about it?" the one standing in the middle says. She's the biggest bitch in the group, so I guess she's the leader.

I laugh again at how ridiculous these girls are. They are all the same. I dealt with these girls every single day when I was a teenager. I did have a bit of a temper. I tended to punch them right in the face and be done with it. I didn't argue; I just shut them up. My parents wanted me to be this meek little girl who would do their every bidding, but that is not me. "Why don't you come over here and we can see." I smile at them. I haven't had a good fight in a while.

The leader steps forward and takes a swing at me. I move my head to the side. Then I whip my head back and smile. "Let's get it." I punch her in the nose, and her head whips back and she holds her face.

"You bitch," she screeches, her teeth bloody. She runs toward me and I punch her again, on the side of her face. She falls to the ground. The other two girls run straight for me. I duck to the side, and one runs into the wall. I grab the other by her hair, tilt her head to the side, and punch her repeatedly in the face. She screams and scratches, trying to get me to let her loose.

The girl on the ground is trying to get up, and I kick her in the face. Blood and spit fly out of her mouth. My fist is still in the other girl's hair. I spin her around and slam her face into a stall door; then I let her go and she hits the ground.

I am tackled from the side, and I catch myself on a stall door. I grab the girl by the throat and drag her closer.

"Let me go, you stupid bitch!" she screams, punching me in the tit.

"The tit, really?" I drag her over to the toilet. I lift the seat with my foot and I push her head into the toilet. I have always wanted to do this. I flush the toilet, and she screams. "Breathe before the water rises."

"What the fuck are you doing, Bailey." I let her go and spin around to face Travis, who is staring at me and the girl.

"Uhh…" I start.

"All three of them tried to attack me, and Bailey intervened," Adeline says. "Then they attacked her, but Bailey destroyed them." She laughs, holding her face.

Smiley pulls her hand away, and I can see the redness on her cheek. "They fucking hit you?" I ask.

She nods and everyone snarls. "Which bitch was it!" I hiss and step out of the stall. She points to the head bitch. Ohh, I don't like that. I run back into the bathroom and grab the top of the toilet tank, ready to bash her head in.

Travis grabs the back of the toilet from me and throws it to the floor. "You're vicious." He laughs and kisses the side of my head. "Come on, they got what they deserved," he tells me and I let out a deep breath, trying to calm myself. We leave the girls in the bathroom and join Travis's friends at the bar.

I sit down in a chair, rubbing the back of my neck. I can't believe I just got into a fight, and with three girls, mind you! Back when I was high school, girls tried to jump me every single day, so I did whatever I could to protect myself.

When Adeline approaches, I sit up and she hugs me tightly. "Thank you so much, sweetheart."

My nose starts stinging from unshed tears. "I got your back." I hug her back and she lets me go, and Smiley immediately snatches her up into his arms. I look down at my hand; my knuckles are bloody.

"Damn, killer. Remind me to not fuck with you," Tristan jokes and I crack a smile.

"I don't like to fight, but I will protect those I care about." I smile at Adeline. I love her like I would love my mother if she weren't such a bitch.

"That's how we all are," Smiley tells me.

Travis comes back and hands me an icepack. He cradles my face in his hand, and I lay my head against his side.

"I think she could give Shaylin a run for her money," Adeline says, and all of the guys look at me with wonder. Travis just laughs loudly and I grin. I can't help it. My temper rarely shows up, but in cases like this it gets the best of me. I just have a huge protective instinct. I want to make sure my family and those I care about are safe.

A door slams, and we all turn to see the girls walking out of the bathroom, looking rough. Three guys get out of their seats and walk over to them. I look at Travis, and he looks at me with the same thought. Uh oh.

The three guys turn to look at us and make their way over. I never expected my first date to be like this.

Travis stands up, and I stand up with him. "Stay behind me, Momma."

Adeline takes my hand and stands next to me as our guys step in front of us to face their adversaries. "This them, Becky?" The man on the right asks. They are dirty and grimy. They all look like they haven't showered since god knows when. Why are these girls with them? They aren't bad looking women, and I am sure they can do better than that.

"Yes." The leader of the group, who I now know is Becky, says in her shrill voice. I take that back—she can't do any better.

"Hand over the bitch that fucked them up, and that will solve all our problems," one of them says, staring at me. I swallow hard, fear taking a hold of me. What do they mean, hand me over?

"That is not going to fucking happen," Travis snarls. I jolt at the sound of his voice. He is scary. I notice the guy closest to me is looking behind me. I turn around just as one of their members, who we didn't notice, sneaks up behind me.

"Travis," I whisper as the man's hand wraps around my arm. Travis spins around, grips his fingers, and twists them back until they break. The guy lets me go and screams, clutching his hand. Travis wraps his arm around my middle and lifts me off the ground. He sets me down against the wall with Adeline. The guys move back in front of us, but this time no one can sneak up behind us.

"You guys are going to regret this." The one standing in the middle points right at me. In a blink of an eye Travis has his gun out, pointing right at his face.

"Mind yourself, you stupid motherfucker. Do you want war?" His body stiffens with anger. I press my hand against his back, and I can feel myself shaking. This is a scary situation. It's one thing to face a bunch of girls, but these guys? What would they do to me if they did get me?

The guy smiles, his yellow-filmed teeth making me sick. Travis presses his hand to my back, and I let out a breath. This is his way of saying he's got me. "War is what you guys will have. Watch your back, bitch." He tells me.

They all glare at me. Travis starts to charge them, but Tristan and I hold him back. They turn around and walk out of the building, the door slamming shut behind them. Travis turns around and tucks me tightly against his chest. "Tell Lane what the fuck just happened, they have it out for us. This is not just about Bailey. They originally sought out Adeline," he tells Smiley, who nods then takes out his phone. Travis looks down at me. "You will be fine, you will be safe. Those fuckers will never touch you."

I nod and close my eyes. This has been one of the best and worst dates of my life, the best because it's with Travis and the worst because someone wants to hurt me. Just my luck, right?

"The others will be here any minute," Smiley tells Travis and the others, but I don't move from his chest. His hands are running up and down my back, and I shiver at the feel of him moving against me. Travis sits down and pulls me onto his lap. Walker and Tristan are staring at the door, and I can see they are majorly pissed off. Smiley is holding Adeline tightly; they are such a beautiful couple. From the moment I met them, I knew I wanted that kind of love someday. The way he took care of her was something I had never seen before.

A few minutes later the door opens, and Lane walks in with a bunch of other members I don't know yet. Smiley steps away from Adeline, and I get off of Travis to allow him to go to the others. "I will be back in a few, sweetheart." He kisses the side of my head, and Adeline joins me.

"He will protect you. Don't worry about a thing, sweetheart." She takes my hand and gives it a comforting squeeze.

"I know he will." I have never felt unsafe around him.

Travis explains what happened and, one by one, they all look at me, shocked. Travis, on the other hand, has a smirk on his face.

"I think you've got some admirers," Adeline teases and I laugh slightly.

"I've just got a temper."

"Mhm. You are made to be a part of the MC life. Mind you, I am not much of a fighter, but I take care of everyone—that's my role."

I smile. "You're everyone's mom." I lean over and hug her.

"Thank you, baby." She rubs the back of my head, and I close my eyes, wishing once again my mother were like her. I miss her. I wish she were there when I had Gabby. One of the nurses held my hand and stayed with me the whole time. That was so amazing of her—otherwise I would have been completely alone.

Travis breaks away from the group of guys and walks over to me. "You ready to go home, baby?"

I nod, getting off the chair, and he takes my hand. I am tired. It's been a long night; it's dragged on since everything went down.

Everyone follows us out of the bar, and Travis approaches his bike. "You will ride in front of me. I don't want your back exposed."

"But won't yours be exposed?"

He gives me a look. "Momma, it's my job to protect you." I hold my hands up in defeat. I know when to pick my battles and when to let them go, and I know that he is serious about being protective.

One of the guys stands at my back while Travis gets on his bike. "I'm Bailey, it's nice to meet you."

He smiles. He has that geeky bad boy vibe that we all love. "My name is Aiden. I'm one of the new members."

Travis looks over at us. "He just got patched in last week."

I smile. "Well, congrats on that."

His smile is utterly sexy. "Why thank you, sweetheart." He winks at me for good measure. Uhh...this one is completely dangerous, I do believe, but Travis is more dangerous to me. He has already stolen a huge piece of me.

"Back the fuck off, Aiden," Travis says in a growl that goes straight down to my lady bits.

Aiden takes a step closer to me. "Or what? This fine lady might want to ride with me." He tilts his head to the side, studying me. I can tell he is fucking with Travis, so I laugh out loud.

"You want me to fucking show you?" Much to my utter surprise, Travis takes his gun out.

Aiden laughs out loud. "Well shoot me if you want, fucker, I'm just messing with you. She knows I'm joking." He keeps on laughing.

Travis puts his gun back, takes my arm, and pulls me toward him. "Put your leg over here." He pats the seat, and soon I am sitting in front of him. "Just lean back and hold on for the ride," he whispers into my ear. The double meaning sends a shiver right down my spine. Oh boy.

He turns on the bike and, one by one, the others do the same. Smiley pulls up with Adeline sitting in the same fashion as me. They are such a hot older couple; I hope I look like that when I am older. Lane raises his hand and takes off, the others following suit. I notice, right off the bat, that they are trying to keep Travis and Smiley in the middle, to protect us. How freaking amazing are these guys?

I never even knew people like this existed. Here I am, my world completely changed. It's like I am fated to be here. One day I was a makeup artist struggling to feed myself, and now I am here in a beautiful home. The most amazing part is Travis; he is surprising me at every turn.

People stop to stare as we drive past; they are in awe of all of these men. I do not blame them; they have a way of commanding everyone's attention. Hell, even Adeline has a way of getting everyone to stop and stare at her. It's the way she carries herself. Joslyn is absolutely beautiful, and I can tell she has a beautiful heart too.

My hair is flying out behind me. I wrap it around my hand and hold it so it's not in Travis's face. He takes my hand in his and wraps my arm around my chest, crossing his arm over it, so my arm and his are hugging my front. *He is holding me.* I close my eyes, enjoying this beautiful moment of being completely and utterly free. My heart and soul feel free. I have found where I am meant to be: right here.

We slow down at the gate to our community. It opens and slams shut behind us. He pulls into my driveway and turns off the bike, and I climb off first. Travis holds my hand, and we walk into the house.

Wilder and Joslyn are sitting on the couch. Wilder gets up and takes Travis into the kitchen, and I sit on the couch with Joslyn. I accidentally brush my knuckles against the couch, and I hiss and look at my hand.

"Woah slugger, what did you do?" Joslyn touches the side of my hand. I hesitate; I don't want people to think I am this really angry person who just wants to fight. I am just extremely protective.

"Three women cornered Adeline in the bathroom." I wait for her reaction.

She laughs. "You go, girl. Adeline didn't deserve that."

I nod. "She really didn't. How was Gabby?" I am dying to go upstairs and check on her.

"She is an absolute angel! Anytime you need someone to watch her, I am more than willing." Joslyn beams.

"Thank you so much. I am here to babysit your babies any time too." I scoot to the edge of the couch. "I need to go see my baby. I will be back." It takes everything in me not to run. I push open her door; she is asleep holding the bunny rabbit that Travis got her the other day. I walk to the edge of the bed and bend down, pressing a kiss to the top of her head.

Her eyes open. "Hi, Momma." My heart swells. I will never grow tired of hearing her call me that.

"Hi, sweet baby. Did you have fun?"

"Lots." She yawns and smacks her lips. She is so adorable. "Go back to sleep. Pancakes for breakfast in the morning?"

She nods. "Please."

I laugh and kiss her cheek. "Goodnight, baby."

"Night, Momma."

I walk into my bedroom. I need to get out of these clothes, which are covered in bar grime and god-knows-what from those hoe bags, and into some sweatpants and a baggy T-shirt.

When I walk downstairs, Travis is sitting on the couch, and Joslyn and Wilder have left. Travis pats the place beside him. I sit down and he wraps his arm around me. He is so warm. I close my eyes for a second, just enjoying the moment.

"Long night, huh?" He runs his hand up and down my back before making his way to my hair, rubbing my scalp.

"It was a good night, no matter what," I say.

"Thank fuck, Momma." You couldn't stop the smile on my face no matter what. I love it when he calls me that. "I am going to run next door to get some clothes, and I will be right back. Lock the door behind me. Until this threat is dealt with, I will be staying here." He says this in a tone that dares me to argue, and you know what? I am not going to.

"Alright." I shrug. He's staring at me in disbelief, but I pretend to not notice. But I notice everything. I noticed that smile he just had on his face. I did that. Yeah, that makes me feel like a million bucks. I follow him to the door.

"See you in a few." He winks and leaves, taking my breath with him.

Travis

What a fucking night. I never expected for it to turn out this way. I knew something was fucking wrong when they never came back from the bathroom. Then I saw Adeline waving for us.

I saw three girls walk into the bathroom after that, and I was fucking paranoid. My first instinct was *they better not have fucking touched her*. She is too sweet for that.

What I never expected was for her to fight like that. She even flushed one of their heads in the toilet. But I am fucking proud of her, sticking up for Adeline and herself. She doesn't need to take anything from anyone, and I am glad she didn't.

Then little things started happening with her. She is not fighting me anymore, and I am grateful for that. I just want her to be happy. I want to make her happy. I walk inside my house with a fucking smile on my face, knowing that I am going right back to see her.

SIX

Bailey

Once Travis left to go to his house, I went to my bathroom and took off my makeup. A huge part of me wants to go to bed and not think about those guys threatening me.

I also want to watch a movie with Travis; maybe he will cuddle? I go into the kitchen and bring out a snack and a couple of sodas. Just as I set everything on the coffee table, there's a knock at the door.

I let Travis in. He's already changed into a pair of sweats and a shirt. Goodness me, he is beautiful. His eyes are out of this world, such a piercing blue. As he locks the door, he spots the food on the coffee table.

"Movie night?" I ask, trying to hide my shaking hands.

"I love that, Momma." He sets his bag down, walks over to the couch, and just sits down so casually. How can he be so casual? I wish I were that relaxed. I feel like screaming half the time. I let out a deep breath; then I sit beside Travis and grab a bag of potato chips and a soda.

"Scary movie?" He picks up the remote and turns on *The Conjuring*. I swallow hard. Should I mention that I am easily scared? I still run down the hallway in fear of something grabbing me. "Sure." I shrug. He turns it on and settles deeper into the couch. I pray that this movie is not terrifying.

Ohhh, it's bad alright. I've already discarded my snacks and am hiding under the blanket, making sure all my body parts are covered. I don't want to be dragged down to the basement. I jump at a scary part and scoot over against Travis. He laughs loudly and puts his arm around me. "I will protect you, baby," he teases, holding me close.

The little girl is getting dragged—oh my God! "Poor little girl," I whisper.

Travis's body starts shaking from laughing at me. "Baby, it's not real." He kisses the top of my head, and I look up at him. When he meets my eyes, my heart starts pounding. Look away, Bailey! But I can't; my eyes are locked into his. His hand cups my jaw, his thumb stroking my cheekbone. I lick my lips and he lowers his head. Is this really happening?

His lips touch mine. I open my mouth and he takes control of the kiss. His lips are full and so freaking soft, so different from any kiss I have had before—this is fire. I press myself closer to him, kissing him back with everything in me. My heart is pounding so hard I am sure he can feel it.

His hand slips from my face to my hips, and I am lifted off the couch until I am straddling him. I feel him. He is rock hard under me. The second thought that crosses my mind: wow, he is big! The third: I want him to take me.

Travis's lips move across mine like he is making love to me, so sweet, hard, and fucking sexy at the same time. I will never be the same after this kiss. I've been wanting to do this since the moment I saw him shirtless.

I hold my breath as I sneak my hand under his shirt. I shiver, goosebumps covering my arm. His abs make me want to drool; they are something you only see on TV. His lips move from mine, and I take in a deep breath. My eyes are still clenched closed, and his hands drift down to my ass and squeeze. Just a little movement of my hips, and I know that I will be pure mush. It's been five years since I've had male contact, and let me tell you, Randall absolutely sucked in bed.

I am sick to my stomach even thinking about it. He was handsome, and that was all there was to him. Selfish, evil, manipulative, and so much more.

Travis's lips are down to my neck. My toes curl and I can't help but rub my clit gently on his dick through his sweats. I feel his teeth drag across my collarbone. I jolt and

I am shaking at this point. I need so much, but I don't know how to ask for it. Do I even want to?

He finally tears his lips from my neck and looks into my eyes. "Fucking beautiful." I smile, lower my face, and wrap my arms around his neck. He shifts his bottom half, and his dick rubs against me. I moan slightly before I catch myself.

"Want to go upstairs?" I ask, my voice almost hoarse, and I am instantly terrified because *what made me ask that?* Oh, I know. I am a horny bitch who wants to get some dick.

His eyes search my face. "You want this?" he asks, and my heart settles down, because that is why I am sure. He is sweet and kind and wants to make sure I am okay. He is all about me; he has done absolutely nothing but focus on my needs.

My lips twitch before I let my smile free. "Yeah, Travis." I touch the side of his face. One part of me is afraid; I don't want to give him the wrong impression. I climb off his lap, he takes my hand, and together we go up the stairs to my bedroom. He smirks as he shuts and locks my door. Oh my god, am I really going through with this?

He walks over to me, and his hand cups the back of my neck. He pulls me to him, pressing his lips to mine again. This kiss is different— this one is setting fire to my soul. My toes curl into the carpet, and I grip the front of his shirt. He pushes me back until my legs hit the bed; then he stands back and looks at me. "Are you nervous?" he asks.

I am on edge. "Yeah," I whisper. I breathe deeply, trying to calm my nerves. "It's been five years, and I've only had sex a handful of times." I throw it out there for him to take as he will. Randall never even gave me an orgasm. Honestly, he was very unkind during sex. It never once felt great and it hurt. He never cared about me or how I felt, only about himself. But the sad part was I thought that was the way life was supposed to be.

Travis's face softens and he cups my jaw. "Don't be scared. I got you, Momma." He stops, his jaw tightening with anger. "I have you now, never be scared with me. I will fucking show you. I will not only protect you physically, I will protect you emotionally, spiritually. Every single part of you. I will take care of you. Your every want will be met and I will fucking give you the world." He kisses my forehead, searing the moment into my mind forever.

Don't cry, Bailey. But it is so hard not to. He touched a huge part of me. I am scared, but he is making that okay. "Thank you." A tear falls down my face. "You're the most amazing person I have ever met in my life." I lean forward and kiss him again, this time with so much emotion. I want to say so much, but I just can't.

His fingers tug on the bottom of my shirt, and I lift my arms as he pulls it over my head, leaving me in my black lace bra. He smiles, dragging his finger down my arm and under my breast, down to my belly button. I suck in a sharp breath as his touch leaves tingles in its wake. His hand is on my back; then his fingers are on my bra clasp.

My insides feel like they are shaking from nerves. My bra comes loose and falls to the floor. I watch as his eyes take me in, and it takes everything in me not to cover myself.

"Beautiful." His fingers lightly graze the side of my breast. "Perfection."

My face is hot. I have never been examined like this. "Lie back, Momma." I do as he asks. His hands grasp the top of my sweatpants. I lift my hips, and he pulls my sweats down my body, taking my panties with them—leaving me completely bare to him. I want to cover myself. His nose flares as he takes in all of me, and his hands grip my hips. "You're the most beautiful fucking thing in the world." His voice is deeper than usual.

"Thank you." He smiles beautifully. It's hard to believe this person is here in front of me. "I think you're overdressed." I lean forward and unbuckle his belt. He lets me unbutton his pants, and I tug them down his legs and pull his boxers off with them. My eyes widen at the size of his dick, and my mouth dries. He is huge and I don't think that's going to fit.

"What?" he asks, touching the bottom of my chin.

I manage to collect myself. "You're huge."

He laughs with that cocky little smirk on his face. Pun is totally intended there—he has the right to be that way. I sit back and watch him take off the rest of his clothes, trying not to be overly aware of my body, naked in front of him. I think of all of the parts of me that are far from perfect. There are the stretch marks on my stomach, and my boobs aren't as great as they used to be. But the way he is looking at me is so full of respect, and it's like he actually thinks I am beautiful.

"Crawl up to the head of the bed," he tells me. I scoot back and he crawls up the bed with me; my heart is pounding so hard. I am so unbelievably nervous. The nervousness is gone the second his lips touch mine. I close my eyes, dragging my hands up his arms, my back hitting the bed. His hands are running all over my body. It's like sensory overload. My pussy is aching and dying for him, and his hands are drifting along my inner thighs.

I open my eyes when he pulls back and kisses my forehead. He kisses my cheek then to the nape of my neck. His lips seem to be touching every nerve ending, and his mouth keeps drifting further down. His lips wrap around my nipple, and I throw my head back, hissing, the pleasure shooting straight down to my clit.

His hand is snaking closer and closer to the spot where I need it. His head moves to one breast as he pinches the other. My back arches, and I can feel myself shaking already. This is so intense that just being near him has me ready to explode. He kisses further down my belly until his mouth is right above my pussy. Wait, is he going to…

"What are you? Nobody…" I stop. His face reddens instantly. "Worthless piece of shit," he snarls when he figures out that nobody has ever went down on me before, and his arms curl around my legs.

His eyes connect with mine just as he dips his head and takes the first lick. "Oh god." I close my eyes and bury my hand in his hair. His arms tighten around me, and he pulls me harder against him. He licks, sucks, bites. My legs are shaking uncontrollably at this point, my fingers buried deep into my sheets. He lets go of one of my legs then puts two fingers inside me and curls them. That's all it takes. I fall over the edge, practically screaming. My whole body is shaking, and I can feel myself pulsating around his fingers. Holy heck, did that just happen?

He rolls a condom on and climbs back on the bed, between my legs. I throw one leg over his back. "Ready, Momma?" He places his forehead against mine. I nod, closing my eyes. I am so ready for this. I feel the tip as he slowly starts entering me, and I relax and allow myself to adjust. Then he stops moving. "Still good?"

"More than good," I whisper, my voice quivering. He slides the rest of the way in and kisses me, moving slowly inside me. His hands run up my sides until he finds my hands, and he places them above my head. His eyes connect with mine as he moves gently and carefully, tenderly. My eyes fill with tears as it hits me. We are making love.

He kisses the tear away and rests his forehead against mine once again. We are just feeling, enjoying, and letting the world fall apart. We are completely one in this moment, and I know I will never doubt him again. He is giving me more than words; he is showing me. Minutes later, we come together as one and, in that instant, our worlds have completely changed.

seven

Bailey

I wake up to the most amazing feeling in the world. Travis has his head on the pillow, and his arm is wrapped around my stomach, holding me tightly.

This is the life. I turn my head and I see it's eight o'clock. Gabby will be getting up very soon, and I need to shower. I tilt my head and stare at Travis. He looks so much younger when he sleeps, but he is just as beautiful.

Last night was something I'd never expected, but it was so much more than I'd hoped for. He showed me something I'd never dreamed of. I felt an amazing connection with someone, and when we had sex I was at the center of it all. He was so intent on making sure I was okay, and he made sure I was having a good time. Last night changed my whole world.

I am so glad that I decided to give him a chance. I never want him to leave. I know it's too soon to say that, but he has been a part of my life from the very moment I met him. He has never once left my side. He was there with me when Gabby had surgery. He stepped up and did whatever he could for me.

I looked for his bad qualities and waited for the other shoe to drop, but it never did. He showed me that not every man is the same, and he is in a league of his own.

I feel him stir beside me, and his eyes slowly open and connect with mine. A slow smile covers his face. "Good morning, Momma." His voice is raspy from sleep.

"Good morning." I rub the back of his head, dragging my nails just slightly. He lifts his head and kisses me softly. I wrap my arms around his neck, hugging him to me. "Gabby will be up soon, I need to shower."

He looks up. "We need to shower." He scoots down the bed, and his hand latches onto my foot, dragging my completely naked self toward him. I laugh and grab the blankets to stop my descent. I turn around, squealing, just as Travis takes a bite out of my ass. I laugh loudly, and I turn around and smack his bare ass.

His eyes narrow on and me first thought is *run*. I take off to the bathroom and shut the door, locking it. The doorknob twists. "You going to let me in so I can eat your pussy?" Uh, can I say no to that?

I hurry and turn on the water; then I rush to the door, unlock it, and run back to the shower, pretending that I didn't just lock him out.

I am under the warm spray, letting the water beat down on my back. He opens the glass door and steps inside, naked as the day he was born. He moves closer, gripping my hips. His dick is hard and resting against his stomach. I swallow hard, a knot in my throat. He is just utter perfection; I can't help but repeat that over and over in my head. I tilt my head back, and he grips my face between his large hands. "Beautifulest woman in the world."

My heart does a little flip, and I smile widely. "You're the most perfect man in the world." I throw it out there for him, not afraid anymore. He kisses my head, and I close my eyes and press myself closer to him, just enjoying the skin-to-skin contact. I never knew it would feel like this; it's like a good-for-your-soul feeling. Just being around him makes me I feel amazing on the inside. I am happy.

He opens my shampoo. "Turn around, baby." I turn around and he starts massaging the shampoo into my hair. I close my eyes and pray that I don't lose my shit. No one has ever been so tender and caring toward me. I am sure my mother never did anything like that for me; my nannies did everything. A tear escapes before I can stop it. A lot has happened within the past twenty-four hours. "Turn around."

I do as he asks, letting the spray of the water wash the shampoo out of my hair. "You're the sweetest guy," I whisper, my voice clogged with emotion.

His face softens. "Baby, only to you and Gabby." Can I say *perfect* again?

I lather up my hands with soap and run them down his arms to his chest, then down and down until I wrap my hand around his dick. He throws his head back, and I make sure to wash him thoroughly.

He returns the favor—he washes me, taking his sweet time. "I need you," he growls. I shiver at the sound of his voice. His hands wrap around my hips, lifting me off the ground, and I wrap my legs around his waist. "Fuck a condom," he snarls.

"I am clean and I am on birth control." I would love to feel him without anything between us.

"I am clean, too. I was just checked the other day, actually." He shifts me in his arms, and I feel him at my entrance. He slowly brings me down onto him and presses my back against the shower wall. I lean my head back against the wall, just taking in the pure ecstasy. His lips are biting, kissing, licking my neck as he moves inside me, hitting that spot every single time.

"Oh god." I moan, dragging my nails down his back. He tightens his grip on me and starts to really pound into me. Last night he was super gentle; this is different. This is hard, all-consuming fucking that sets you on fire.

"Ready to come for me, Momma?" he grinds out through clenched teeth, and I tighten around him, my toes curling. I lean forward and bite his shoulder, trying not to scream and wake Gabby up. I feel him come inside me. I shiver and he moves into the spray to warm me up.

My head is tucked into the side of his neck. His hand is moving up and down my back, caressing me. He is so strong; he is holding me up practically with one arm. "I don't know about you, but I am starving." I murmur against his neck, my growling stomach making itself known.

He laughs, "I think we need to feed you and the baby girl."

Baby girl? I absolutely love that he called Gabby that! I love the way he has been involved with Gabby from the start.

We finish showering and walk downstairs. I open the refrigerator and grab some bacon. I wish I was the mom who could make everything from scratch, but I didn't get that talent. Travis pitches in, and we work as a team making breakfast. I lean against the counter watching him flipping the bacon. He looks over at me, smiling. "See something you like?" he teases.

I bite my lip, making sure he sees me checking him out. He laughs, grabbing my hand and pulling me toward him, and kisses me on the lips. I hear a giggle, and I pull back and see Gabby standing at the entrance to the kitchen. "Good morning, baby."

She is smiling ear-to-ear. Her hair is an absolute mess, and I know it's going to be a pain to fix it. "Morning, Momma and Ravis." I love how she can't exactly say *Travis*.

"Good morning, baby girl, breakfast is ready," Travis says. My poor little heart surely can't stand much more. She beams at him and sits at the table. I wish I had her energy in the morning. She is rarely in a bad mood and is such a happy little girl. Just being around her makes everything better. She is a beautiful light in this fucked-up world.

Travis is another beautiful light. He and Adeline gave me hope when I had none; then my whole life completely changed.

Travis fixes a plate for Gabby while I serve our food. I love that he is putting her first and making sure she has everything she needs. "Do you want milk?" He cranes his neck around the wall so he can see her.

"Yes, thank you."

I smile.

Travis looks at me, shaking his head. "She is absolutely precious, her manners. You did good, Momma."

That felt amazing; no one has ever said anything like that to me before. I never knew how much I wanted to hear it. "Thank you." I walk over and kiss him hard on the lips. He smacks me hard on the butt, and I yelp and pull away.

I grab our plates and walk toward Gabby, who is sitting waiting, her legs swinging under the table. "What do you want to do today?" I ask her. She hasn't been out much since her surgery. We all sit down, with her at the head of the table, and Travis slides her plate and a glass of milk in front of her.

"Thank you." She smiles at him. She steals everyone's hearts; she stole mine the moment I found out

I was pregnant with her. "Can we go to a toy store?" she asks hesitantly.

"I bet they have that doll you've been wanting." I wink at her. She has been wanting a doll that is a lot like a real baby.

She gasps dramatically. "You really fink so?"

"Yes baby, but you need to eat and then we can get dressed to go."

She grabs her fork and digs into her food.

"You know you're more than welcome to come, Travis," I say.

His face softens. "I know, baby."

I take a bite of my pancake so he doesn't see my goofy grin, and Travis just watches both of us and shakes his head. He doesn't bother hiding his absolutely beautiful smile.

Gabby and I decided to wear matching outfits today. We are both wearing a pair of boyfriend jeans and a loose T-shirt, with our hair curled around our faces.

I love that she wants to dress like me, and I know it won't be like this when she's older, so I am going to enjoy every single moment of it. Travis is getting ready in my room. He's basically moved into my room since we had sex. It's kind of hard to wrap my head around the fact that I actually had sex. It's not like I hadn't done it, but this was so absolutely amazing I'm kind of in a state of shock.

"Ready, baby?"

Gabby finishes looking at herself in the mirror. She is such a mini-me. She runs over and grabs my hand. "We look nice, Momma."

I laugh. "We sure do, baby." We walk hand-in-hand down the stairs. Travis is already down here, putting his shoes on. He looks up and whistles. "Aren't you ladies just beautiful. Are you sure you want this peasant to come along with you?"

Gabby laughs loudly and I join her, shaking my head.

"Ravis, you're funny."

He winks and opens the front door.

"Hang on, let me grab my purse," I tell him, and he reaches out and grabs my hand, stopping me. I eye him. "What?"

"You won't need it. I got this."

My mouth opens and closes a few times. "But Travis…" I start to argue, but he just leans in and kisses the shit out of me.

"You have done a lot, Momma, let me do this." His voice is soft, kind of raw with emotion. I search his face for any sign of hesitation, but he has none.

"Okay." I want to say no and stomp my foot, but I know when to back down.

"Good girl."

I groan internally, and my thoughts immediately go to sex. He has that smirk on his face, and he knows exactly what he is doing to me. He opens the door, and Gabby and I walk out onto the porch.

I look at the surrounding houses. "Do all of these houses belong to the MC?"

"Yes, most of the single guys and some family members live here. The families usually build their house on the property we bought outside of town. It's very secluded, and the only neighbors are MC members." He locks the door.

It's amazing that everyone is so close, and they are always there for each other; it gives me a safe and warm feeling. They are like a family. I am glad that Travis had all of this.

He unlocks the truck.

"I need to get the car seat out of the SUV."

"You don't need to, I bought one for my truck." Here I am once again completely floored. He thinks of things most men never would. He is one of a kind and I can't believe he is kind of mine.

"You're amazing," I tell him, and he kisses my temple.

"Only to my girls." Well, there goes my heart; it just shattered into a million little bits, and I know that I will never be the same. I never want to be the same. I would not change a thing.

I stop walking and just watch them together. He lifts her into the truck, and I watch them talk while he is putting her into her seat. Our worlds have changed in such an amazing way. I remember going to sleep every single night praying for a miracle to come into my life. I just thought, maybe a better job? I never expected two hundred and thirty pounds of pure man to come into my life and show me something different. I break out of my Travis fog and get into the passenger seat. I look back at Gabby, who is swinging her little legs. Travis gets in and turns on the radio to country music. "Let's hit the road." He puts on his sunglasses and rolls all the windows down. Oh boy.

We arrive at the toy store, and it's absolutely huge. Gabby screams from the back seat. Travis laughs and gets out. He walks around and opens my door then hers.

He sets her on the ground, and she starts jumping. "So excited," Travis says. He takes her hand. "How fucking cute." I nod and take her other hand, and we walk hand-in-hand into the store.

"Oh my goodness!" Gabby practically screams, and I laugh at how excited she is. She pulls us along as we go through every single aisle until we find the doll. She stops dead in her tracks, her eyes wide and mouth open.

"I guess they have it?" Travis asks me, and I point.

Gabby shakes our hands loose and sprints to the middle of the aisle. She grabs the doll and hugs it to her chest. "Finally, Momma's got you," she coos to the doll.

Travis stares down at her for a few beats, then at me. "My heart can't take it."

I laugh because he is feeling what I am feeling. "I know."

Gabby looks up and gasps at all the baby beds, strollers, high chairs, and clothes designed for her doll. She puts her hand over her mouth; did I mention my daughter is a bit dramatic?

Travis bends down next to her. "I think your baby needs all of this to properly care for it, don't you think?" She nods, and for the next hour I watch them interact with each other. He goes through every single article of clothing she may want for her baby. He is getting her every single item. I don't even want to know how expensive this is, but he is enjoying this as much as she is.

She is on top of the world. He is making her feel so important, making sure her opinion on everything matters. He even got a worker to bring a buggy to carry everything, which is a lot mind you. "Fank you sooo much, Ravis." She runs over and jumps on him, he catches her, and she wraps her arms around his neck.

Travis

This is heaven: Gabby's arms around my neck, hugging me. My eyes are closed as I enjoy this moment.

I wanted to spoil her; I wanted her to get everything she has ever wanted. They both deserve the fucking world.

When I open my eyes, Bailey is holding her chest and staring at both of us with an expression on her face I have never seen before. She is affected, and I am affected. Gabby has stolen my heart, and I consider her mine. I want her to be my daughter. I want her mom to be mine.

"Did you know they just opened a new trampoline place next door?" I ask Gabby.

She looks up at me, her eyes bright with happiness. "Oh, can we go, Ravis?" I look at Bailey and she rolls her eyes before nodding.

"Yes we can, angel." I tell her.

I run my hand down the back of Gabby's head, and she dramatically throws her arms around me again. "Oh Ravis, you're the best!" she screams, half deafening me, and I laugh, hugging her back. "Anything for you, angel."

Bailey

She is in little-girl heaven. Travis paid for me and him to jump too, but we just like watching her bounce all over the place. She climbs the rock wall and bounces around like a little monkey.

"Mommy, will you climb the rock wall? Puhlease?" she begs, her big brown eyes wide.

"I will try it, baby." I allow the guy to strap me into the harness.

Travis is watching me, grinning ear-to-ear. "You got this, Momma."

I laugh nervously. "I am not sure about that, I am scared of heights." I begin my ascent, and halfway up I get stuck. I can't reach the next handle. I start to panic; my whole body is shaking.

"You okay, baby?" Travis asks, and I shake my head. No, I am not okay.

Travis

She is fucking terrified; I can see her shaking from here. "Baby, can you slowly climb down, or jump down?"

She starts to climb down, but stops. "I am just going to let go." She lets go, and I see the worker release the rope and run off. I run over and grab the rope, and it burns my hands as I stop her from free falling to the ground. She looks at me, holding the rope, completely terrified. I let go and the skin on my hands is completely torn to shreds.

She covers her mouth; then she plays it cool because Gabby is watching.

"Woah, Momma, you went down super fast! How fun." She doesn't know that her mom almost fell twenty feet.

Bailey closes her eyes, holding her chest. I pull her into my arms. "Come here, Gabby." I say gently. I need to make sure she is close to me. The worker purposely walked away. He wanted her to get hurt, and I am going to get to the bottom of it. That is for sure.

Bailey

Breathe, I repeat to myself over and over. I am sick to my stomach; my worst fear just happened. From the corner of my eye, I saw the worker running away. Travis saved me from being seriously hurt or even killed. I am shaking to the point that I can barely stand. He kisses my forehead. "Let's get out of here," he whispers, and he lets me go and helps me out of my harness. I grab Gabby; I want her close in case it really was intentional. I don't want her to leave my side until I am sure about that.

I notice Travis's hands. "You're hurt," I choke out. The skin on his hands is completely torn and bleeding. It hurts me to see them in such bad shape.

He shakes his head. "This is nothing, baby." He throws the harness away. He takes my hand and then Gabby's, and we walk out of the building. I just want to go home and snuggle on the couch. Just forget that horrible experience. I am never doing anything like that again.

We are at the edge of the sidewalk in front of the building when a car with very dark tinted windows speeds toward us. Travis picks up Gabby, wraps his arm around me, and pulls me back. The vehicle pulls out into traffic, almost hitting another vehicle, and then it's gone.

"What the fuck is happening?" I say out loud.

"We need to get out of here." Travis pulls me tightly to his side and clutches Gabby against his chest. He practically carries me right along with Gabby. He opens my door and I get inside, and he puts Gabby in her seat.

I lean back to buckle her in. The moment his door is shut, the same vehicle comes back around. A window rolls down; a gun is peeking out. I jump over the back of the seat and lie on top of Gabby just as the gun goes off, hitting her window. I look at the window in absolute shock; it's bulletproof. I close my eyes and cry. I thought I was going to lose my baby.

Travis is out of the car, with his gun out, sprinting after the vehicle. He fires three shots in quick succession. Pop! Pop! Pop! The vehicle crashes into a light pole.

Travis

What-the-ever-fuck is happening? The guy pulls his gun out, and I am already out of my car. I hear the gun going off, and I'm flooded with anger unlike any I have ever felt before.

The bullets hit Gabby's window; these fuckers are aiming for her. It makes me so fucking thankful we reinforced all of our vehicles to make them as safe as possible. Bullets can't penetrate them.

I catch up to the car and empty my clip, taking out all the tires and shooting toward the back of his head. His vehicle runs headfirst into a light pole, and I run over and whip the fucker out of the truck. He hits the ground, screaming. I take the mask off of his face, and he is holding his hands up. I recognize him immediately. This is one of the fuckers from the bar.

I take out my phone and hit the alert button, sending out my location and letting my brothers know I need them. These guys are going to fucking suffer. They are going to fucking more than suffer. I will make sure they beg for their lives, but their begging will be futile. They tried to hurt Bailey and then her daughter, my daughter. That shit is unforgivable.

I keep my gun trained on him, and I look back at the truck. There are still people in the vehicle, but I can barely see them.

A minute or so later, I hear the bikes, and I close my eyes for a split second. They are coming. I am fucking dying to get to my girls. I want to kill this fucker and take them home, away from all of this bullshit. But this fucker is going to regret his actions. We need to figure out what this little club has planned.

Wilder pulls up next to us, his eyes wide with anger. "What the fuck happened?" I explain everything, and Wilder takes my gun from me. "I got this, get your girls home and we'll see you later." He gives me a look.

I look down at the stupid son of a bitch on the ground. I want to fucking smash his face in. I want to fucking tear him limb from limb.

"I will be seeing you later," I tell him before laughing. I nod at Wilder and run across the parking lot to my truck.

I open the passenger door. Bailey is crying and holding Gabby. "I think Mommy is scared from almost falling, Ravis." Gabby pats her mom on the back. Thank fuck she is young and doesn't understand. I close my eyes. She needs to be sheltered and protected from all the fucking evil in life.

"Scoot over, Momma," I tell her softly. She slides into the middle seat, and I wrap my arms around her and Gabby. Gabby snuggles against my chest, and Bailey lays her head against my arm. Little by little, her crying starts to settle. I see my brothers coming, one by one. "You're safe," I whisper.

She nods. "It just scared me, Gabby could have..."

"Shh. I will always protect you." I kiss the top of her head. She nods and holds onto my arm. "I think we are ready to go home and take a nap, aren't we?" I ask Gabby, whose eyes are drooping. I carefully move her to her seat and buckle her in. I climb over Bailey and start the truck. She stays in the middle seat and places her hand on my leg.

"I am so ready go home." She lays her head on my shoulder. I place my hand on her right leg, holding her as best as I can. She was already fucking rattled after almost falling; then the fucker tried to hit us and shot Gabby's window. I can't stop thinking about the bullets hitting Gabby's window. In a blink of an eye, your whole world can be taken away. My world could have been taken away.

eight

Bailey

A Few Hours Later

I am lying on the couch, a blanket covering my bottom half. You could not take this smile off my face. I am in heaven.

Travis is sitting on the floor with Gabby, playing dolls. He is putting a diaper on the new baby doll, who just pooped fake poop. Gabby is covering her mouth and giggling at Travis, who is pretending to be sick. He re-dresses the baby and hands it to her. "How did I do?" he asks.

She tilts her head to the side, like she is thinking on it. "I think you are doing pretty good, Ravis." She grins at him and pats his forearm. She starts feeding the baby from a bottle. She is so in love with the stuff he has bought her. I love that he got down on her level and played with her;

that is so important. She was surprised that he did that, and she loved the attention. I love to see her so happy. She's only had me all these years. Her dad sure never did anything but be grouchy and want nothing to do with her.

Travis sits down next to me and puts my legs in his lap. I sit up, snuggling closer. Ever since everything happened earlier, I just want to be as close to him as possible. He makes me feel so safe.

"How are you feeling, Momma?" He smooths my hair over my shoulder, looking at me closely.

"I'm okay now, I was just a bit rattled earlier." I am sure he could already guess that from all of the crying I did. Seeing a gun pointing straight at Gabby's window... I could have lost her. Thank goodness the windows were bulletproof.

"It fucking scared me, too. I need to leave in an hour. There will a prospect with you until I get back. We need to figure out what happened." He is watching my reactions to his words.

"Just get those fuckers, they almost hurt my baby." I close my eyes and lean forward until my head is resting on his chest. At that moment, peace comes over me. He is my safety, security, warmth. He is everything I have always needed and never knew I wanted.

"That's for fucking sure, baby," he whispers so Gabby doesn't hear.

Gabby climbs onto the couch and gets between me and Travis. I laugh, and she pulls my blanket over her lap, snuggling into Travis's side. He runs his finger down the side of her cheek. His face is so soft and filled with...love. He loves my baby. That is the most important thing to me. She comes first in my life, always. I love that, from the moment he met us, he has always put her first.

I never doubted that he was hanging around with the best intentions; he is just perfect for both of us. I would be lying if I didn't admit that I was falling for this man, because I am. Hard and fast. Sometimes it just hits me that this is my life, and it's so hard to believe. I went from being so alone to sharing my life with someone.

Travis lifts Gabby onto his lap, holding her like a baby. Gabby giggles, staring up at him. My heart... "I am not a baby, Ravis." She giggles, covering her mouth with her hand.

He smiles widely. "You're my baby, always." He tickles her, causing her to scream with laughter.

"Ravis, stop!" she manages to get out through her laughter, tears falling down her face. He stops, kissing the top of her head. He grabs the blanket, covering her as he would a baby.

"I love you, Ravis," she says so casually, not realizing the full impact of her words and what they do to change lives. Travis looks at me, and I see pure shock on his face. I cover my mouth to stifle my tears. My baby doesn't tell just anyone she loves them. This is huge. He is making a tremendous impact on her life. I just never realized how much until this very moment. She loves him.

Travis bends down and kisses the top of her head. "You know I love you too, right angel?"

She smiles at him. "I know, Ravis." She pats his arm, yawning again, and closes her eyes. He pulls her more tightly against him and runs his fingers down the back of her head. He is staring down at her like his world begins and ends with her. I know the feeling all too well.

I scoot a little closer, resting my head on his shoulder. I want more kids. I want as many as God is willing to let me have.

We sit on the couch, watching TV just like a family would. Gabby is already asleep, and I will be out soon. Today has been mentally exhausting.

Travis

Both of them are asleep. I lay Gabby down on the couch and tuck the blanket in around her, and I place a pillow on the floor in case she falls off.

I lean down and kiss Bailey on the lips. "Baby," I whisper, and I push the hair out of her face. Her beautiful eyes open. "I will be back soon, get some rest." She nods, closing her eyes again. I kiss the top of her head and walk outside.

The prospect is sitting on the front porch. I nod at him and get on my bike. Then I head to the club, where the fucker is waiting for me. The moment I sit on my bike, everything changes. The softness leaves me. This fucker needs to pay.

The interrogation room is in the basement. We keep it separate so the screams are not as easily heard.

When I enter the room, the guy is sitting down and his arms and legs are tied to the chair. The other MC members are already here waiting for me. Lane nods at me, giving me full permission to do what is needed.

Someone puts his hand on my shoulder. It's Aiden, and he is pissed. He nods, letting me know that he has my back. All of my brothers do.

I turn my attention to the fucker sitting in the chair, staring at me. I am fucking sick. I grip his face between my hands, squeezing. "Tell me everything I want to fucking know. I will let you die kind of quick, or I can drag it out." I lean in closer, looking him dead in the eye. "Or I can make it last for days, weeks, months. It's your fucking choice. Why did you try to shoot my daughter?"

He throws his head back laughing.

He wants to play it like that? Aiden walks to the wall and grabs some steel knuckles, and I slip them over my fingers. I am not fucking playing; this shit is personal. The sight of the fucking gun pointing straight at Gabby's window will never leave me. Fucking scarred me for life. I could have lost everything before I even had it.

Aiden stands right by my fucking side,

I punch the fucker right on the mouth. That fucking laugh of his was wearing on my last nerve. He stops laughing as blood pours out of his mouth. He spits and teeth hit the ground. I smirk when I see tears in eyes. Yes fucker, cry. He looks at me, and I punch him again, right in the jaw. I hear a sickening crack, and I laugh at his pained-filled expression. Good.

"'Top."

I laugh. "Ohh no, are your teeth hurting? I will fix that for you." As I walk past him, I make sure to tap the side of his jaw where I shattered it. He screams for the first time. Well shit, that barely took any effort at all.

I look back at the guys and they roll their eyes. I can't fucking stand it when they are easy to break. This fucker will be talking any minute now. I walk over to the wall of hell and grab a pair of pliers.

Aiden is bent over, whispering in his ear, and I arch an eyebrow when the fucker turns pale before my eyes. Then I notice his jeans are getting darker around the crotch. Aiden stands back up, grinning ear-to-ear. He is fucking vicious. He may look like a dork with those glasses, but he is fucking Dexter in the flesh.

"Open for me." I wiggle my pliers. His eyes widen and he clamps his mouth shut. "Fine then." I grab the knife resting on the table next to him. Someone must have been fucking with him before I got here, probably Aiden. I use the pliers to grip his lip, then I slide the knife through. He opens his mouth, screaming, and I throw his bottom lip in his lap.

"Fine!" He screams, his words barely coherent, thrashing in his chair.

I take a step back, making a big show of setting the knife down on the table.

"Fucking pussy, I hate when they are weak. They aren't any fun." Aiden laughs. I look at him sideways. I told you the fucker loves this shit.

The guy in question finally looks at me. He tries to grin, but that's kind of fucking hard with your lip gone. "In the beginning it may have been about Adeline, but we had a reason. Do you know how much one of the Grim Sinners' or Devils Souls' kids are worth? You guys have a lot of enemies." I am fucking sick to my stomach. I look at the guys and they are all pale. It's one thing to mess with us, but to know our kids have hits on them? Then it sinks in: he wanted Gabby. "Today was an attempt to grab your daughter, but she wouldn't leave your fucking side. A sweet little thing like that would have made me millions." He shifts in his seat. I look down and see he has an erection. I grab my gun and shoot him. He screams, looking down at his crotch, where I just fucking shot him. Aiden is jumping up and down. We are all fucking pissed.

"Have you sold any girls yet?" I ask. I know they haven't gotten to the MC kids.

He nods.

"Where?" I smack him across the face.

"Forty-three Donna Street, yellow house," he manages to get out, before he passes out from the blood loss. I look at the guys. I am shaking all over. What if that had been Gabby? Do not fucking go there, Travis. She is home safe with her mom. They will not touch a hair on her head, ever. We will put a fucking stop to this; we have a lot of enemies because we will not allow shit like this to go on. Yes, the law is important, but some shit needs to be dealt with another way.

Lane is in the corner, on the phone—probably with Kyle. They need to know what is happening. I can't fucking stand around waiting.

"We will get them, Travis. I fucking promise." Aiden is standing next to me, and he is fucking shaking as much as I am. I look at Lane, who is just as fucking bad because he has an eight-year-old daughter. Wilder, who also has a daughter, is fucking pale. I know in this instant the MCs will come together and we will end all of this. This is not the first time we have taken down shit like this. Being in Texas, close to the border, causes shit like this to happen more often than it should.

Lane puts his phone in his pocket. "Let's ride." I take out my gun and put a bullet in the fucker's head; he doesn't deserve to breathe another fucking second. I want to do so much more damage, but there are other things that need to be done.

We follow Lane out of the basement, and we don't say a fucking word as we get on our bikes. We have just one thing on our minds: we need to get there as fast as we can.

We arrive at the yellow house, and one of the guys is stationed near the back door to make sure someone doesn't try to escape out the back. Lane walks right up and kicks the door. A man jumps off the couch, and Wilder pushes him back down, pointing a gun at him. "Sit fucking still."

I follow Lane down to the basement. It's sad but that is where everyone tends to keep people they have kidnapped. We turn on the light, and lying on a dirty mattress is a baby who couldn't be more than a few months old. The smell hits me next and I gag; it smells like pure shit and piss. We search all over and don't see anyone else. I pick up the baby, tucking him against my chest.

I look at Lane, who is resting his head against the wall. This shit is something we will never forget. When we walk back upstairs, all the guys turn to look at us. The guy sitting on the couch looks at the baby.

"Aww fuck, I just bought him a few hours ago. I didn't touch him, I swear." He holds his hands up in the air. I close my eyes in fucking relief. There are fucking sick people in this world. Thank God this baby is young enough that this shit shouldn't affect him.

"Where is his family?" Lane asks. The guy looks at all of us, way too calm for my liking. Doesn't he know he is not only going to die—he is also going to be a message to that fucking MC? We are coming for them.

"Apparently, he is some homeless woman's baby. She sold him for a few grand of dope." I close my eyes. How can someone do something like this? This baby never had a chance in this world; these people were setting him up for fucking failure from the start. Lane looks at me and at the baby I'm holding. I don't know what to fucking do.

"I will take him with me tonight." Wilder volunteers.

"If Amelia weren't about to give birth, I would," Lane says. "We are going to try to locate his family."

"I will take him," Aiden tells everyone. I turn around and look at him. I never expected that. "Aiden, are you sure?" Lane asks.

He nods. "I always wanted a baby, and I have the space and the means to take care of him." This is very true. Aiden has mentioned to me before that he has always wanted to be a dad, and I have a feeling that we aren't going to find this baby's family.

"Aiden, why don't you come home with me, and we can help you for a few days until you get the hang of it? We have a guest room."

Aiden nods. "That would be great. I know Bailey can help me." He steps closer to me and I give him the baby, who is fast asleep. My heart is fucking hurting at the sight of him. He is so fucking tiny and innocent, and if we hadn't gotten here when we did, everything would have been so different.

Lane grabs the man from the couch by his hair and drags him outside. "Me and you are going to have a talk. I want to know everything."

"Let me call Bailey, we need to grab some stuff for the baby," I tell Aiden, and he nods.

She answers after a few rings. "Hey, baby." I hurry and explain the situation, and I hear her sniff over the phone. I know this shit is hitting close to home because of Gabby.

"She is texting me a list of the basics, we can always grab the other stuff whenever," I tell Aiden.

"I want to thank you, man. This means a lot to me."

"It's nothing, it's what family is for." I smack his shoulder and drag him outside with me. The air has a chill, and the baby starts crying immediately.

"Travis, can you grab me my jacket out of my saddlebag?" Aiden asks me. I grab his jacket and hand it to him.

A prospect drives up in a truck, and Lane looks at Aiden. "Here is your truck, and we had a car seat installed in there."

"Thank you, Lane." Aiden walks over to the truck. I open the door for him, and Aiden puts the baby inside the car seat. He sets his jacket on the seat beside him. I show Aiden how to properly secure it.

"I will follow you to Myra's and then the store." We need to make sure he is okay. Aiden gets in the driver's seat and I get on my bike.

Aiden's entire world just changed, and I know he is going to be an amazing fucking dad. We are all good dads. I just never realized how much I wanted it until Gabby.

nine

Bailey

From the moment I got that call from Travis, it has not left my mind: trafficking? I know things like this happen, but for it to happen here, right under all of our noses?

That is a huge wake-up call. I can't even fathom the mentality of someone who would do something like that. I clench my eyes closed. I don't want to think of things like that.

Travis texted me around twenty minutes ago, letting me know they are leaving the store and heading home. I know they took the baby to Myra.

I hear a motorcycle pull up outside, and I walk to the front door and step out onto the front porch. Aiden gets out of the truck, and Travis opens the door and takes out a ton of bags. I guess they got what I told them to, and a lot more. Aiden shuts the door, carrying a small bundle.

I step aside, holding the door open for him. "You need me to help you carry, Travis?" He shakes his head with a faint smile.

Aiden smiles at me. Okay, Aiden has this sexy geek thing going on. He is completely sleeved out, and his hair is dark brown, gelled slightly to the side but messed up enough to give him that ruffled undone look. Travis sets everything down on the living room floor and goes back outside; my guess is that he's going out for another load. Aiden sits down on the couch with the baby.

"He is beautiful," I say softly." I am itching to hold him. "I miss Gabby being this small." There is nothing better than snuggling with a baby.

"I don't know what to do," he confesses. I laugh.

"I didn't know either, but it eventually becomes second nature. It's not an easy thing to do, but it's so worth it."

"I think that's everything." Travis groans as he carries in the last bag.

I spot the baby bathtub. "I think he needs a bath, some pajamas, and food," I tell Aiden. I search the bag, finding the supplies needed. Travis carries the bathtub into the kitchen, and as I fill the tub, I make sure to show Aiden the correct temperature. Travis is helping him get the baby out of his clothes.

"He needs a name." I can't continue calling him *Baby*.

Aiden tilts his head to the side for a few seconds. "How about Reid?"

I smile. "I love it." I explain to Aiden everything he needs to know, and I drag Travis out of the kitchen, leaving him on his own.

I sit down on the couch, and Travis plops down beside me. "What a day, huh?" I rub my tired eyes.

Travis yawns. "That's for sure."

I bend down and begin taking everything out of the bags. I grab the formula, bottles, and baby food. "How old is he?" I ask Travis.

"He is five months, from what Myra can figure out."

I shake my head. He is so small. "He is underweight, isn't he?"

Travis nods. "Yes he is, but not as bad as she would have expected. She sees nothing wrong with him, but she did do tests. She gave us a special formula to help bring his weight up."

I stare down at the tiny clothes, my heart breaking. "It's so sad, Travis," I whisper, and I lean against him.

"I know, baby." He kisses the side of my head. I let out a deep breath and grab the formula and the bottle. I want to get some food in him as fast as possible.

Aiden looks up as I walk in. "I am afraid I am going to hurt him." Reid is staring up at Aiden like he is trying to understand who he is. He yawns and starts sucking on his hand. How precious.

"You're doing perfectly fine. Is he ready to get out?" I ask.

"I think so." Aiden takes a towel from a pile on the counter, and he takes Reid out of the water. Reid cries from being cold. "Shh, I have you."

My poor little heart. I can't wait to see Travis with his own baby. I want to have a bunch of kids with him.

Travis comes into the kitchen and puts his arm around my shoulders. We stand together watching Aiden, making sure he doesn't need anything. It's really amazing that he would take Reid without hesitation, and I love the fact that you don't have to be in a relationship to be a parent. He is taking on a huge role, and he will be fine.

Aiden finally gets him lotioned, diapered, and dressed, and he tucks him against his chest, smiling. "I'm in love."

Yeah, I understand 100 percent where he is coming from. "Do you need me to help you with the bottle?"

He nods. "Thank you." I lead him through the process and hand him the bottle. He takes it and walks into the living room, and he sits down in the recliner. Travis and I follow and sit down on the couch.

"We need to put together the bed." I tell Travis.

"How about I do it, and you can help fix the room up for Aiden?"

I grab the bags and set the bottles, formula, and water on the table so he can easily grab it tonight. I fix a makeshift changing table, having everything at the ready. I put Reid's clothes and blankets in the chest. Then I fix Aiden's bed for him; he will need as much sleep as he can for the next couple of days until he gets into the swing of things.

I head back downstairs. "Don't forget to burp him every few ounces." I learned that the hard way with Gabby. Travis has Reid's bed set up. It's a simple pop-up one. When Aiden goes home he can get a crib.

Reid starts crying, and Aiden pats him on the back, gently rocking. He is a natural! Travis gets up, carrying the small bed. "I will be back."

I yawn and turn on the TV, and I relax on the couch. Travis comes back and pulls me into his lap, and we watch TV together. From the corner of my eye, I watch Aiden and Reid, but Aiden seems to have it down pat.

"I think I am going to lay him down and sleep myself. Thank you all for everything." Aiden smiles.

"It's nothing, that's what family is for, right?" Travis speaks often of the MC being a family, and I feel like I am a part of that now.

"That's right." Aiden nods and walks up the stairs.

I close my eyes, snuggling into Travis. "Let me clean up the kitchen, and I will be ready for bed." I stare at the baby things, including the little bitty socks. Travis comes up behind me, wrapping his arms around me.

"You miss it, don't you?" he asks.

I nod. "Yes, I do—a lot."

He turns around, looking serious. "Let's have a baby."

My mouth opens. Did he really just say that? "What are you trying to say?"

He smiles, that achingly beautiful smile. "Let's have a baby. I know you're it for me, baby. Why not start now?"

Do I want this? Do I want a baby now with Travis? I throw caution to the wind, and for once I do what I want. "Okay," I whisper. He kisses me hard on the lips. It's sudden, but I can't help it. He has taken over my whole life; I have never felt like this before. I want to experience everything with him. I want Gabby to have a brother or a sister. I want to see Travis hold our baby and Gabby.

"Let's hurry and clean this up so we can get to the baby making," he says in a very country accent. I laugh loudly and wipe everything down while he empties the tub. I stop thinking *do I really want to do this? What if something happens and I am alone again?* I close my eyes thinking, *if worst comes to worst, I can take care of two children myself*—but I don't think that will ever happen. We clean everything up, and Travis follows me up the stairs holding my hand.

Travis shuts the door quietly and locks it. I am already taking off my clothes, no longer ashamed to do so. He leans against the wall, his eyes dark, watching my every movement. I turn around, bending over at the waist, slipping my panties down my legs. "Fuck." I hear him groan, and I grin and turn around, taking my hair out of my bun and letting my curls fan around my face.

One second he is leaning against the door, and the next, his hand is in my hair as he kisses me. Finally. It's like coming home the second his lips touch mine. The world stops—everything stops—and it's just me and him. Kissing him, being with him, is such an amazing feeling.

It's a good-for-your-soul feeling, and I know this is right where I am meant to be. He is what I have needed my whole life, the missing piece to the puzzle.

I grip the bottom of his shirt, and he breaks the kiss long enough so I can pull it over his head. He hands rest on either side of my neck. My eyes connect with his. "We are really doing this?" I whisper. It's really sinking in that this is happening.

His right hand glides up from my neck to my face, cupping my jaw gently. "I've always wanted to be a dad, and Gabby made me want more kids. I feel like Gabby is my own, and I want her to have brothers and sisters to grow up with."

Whatever part of my heart didn't belong to Travis is gone in a split second. His admitting that he feels like Gabby is his is everything to me. She needs and deserves someone like this in her life.

I press my face into his chest. I just want to hold him for a few seconds. He kisses the top of my head. I pull back and unbutton my pants.

"Get on the bed, baby." I climb on the bed, and he pulls his pants down. I am shaking in anticipation of everything that's going to happen; my world is changing so fast. I wouldn't change one thing.

He is so handsome—the way he carries himself and the way he looks at me. He treats me like I am a precious jewel that needs to be protected at all costs. I have never felt so free—and just happy—in my life.

He climbs onto the bed, kissing me deeply. I shiver and lean back into the bed until I am lying on my back. His lips trail to my neck, and I grip the back of his head. He nips, kisses, and licks his way down my body. He grips my hips and, all of a sudden, I am lying facedown. He bites into my ass cheek, and as I look back at him, he looks me in the eye. "Oh god," I moan as his fingers move between my legs. He slips his thumb inside me, and I open my legs wider and tilt my hips toward him.

"Is my Momma hungry for me?" His words are deep, raspy, and oh so sexy.

"Always."

Smack! I jump, my ass stinging from the smack. "On your knees." I do as he asks, and his hands wrap around my thighs, spreading my legs further apart. "Mmm, this is all for me." He groans, and goosebumps break out across my skin at his dirty words.

"Only for you."

He growls. "That's fucking right," he says and his tongue circles my clit, this angle different but oh-so-good. I grip the blankets, burying my face into the pillow, trying to hold myself together. "Mine," he says before sucking hard. I cry out, slamming my hand into the headboard.

"Yours," I breathe out and bite my lip.

"What is it you're wanting, Momma?" he says between licks.

"You."

He stops. I feel him moving behind me, and I look back to see him holding his dick in his hand. How is he so freaking sexy? "You have me," he whispers in my ear, his breath causing me to shiver. He slowly presses himself inside me. "Fucking made for me." He groans, kissing his way down my back. He moves slowly, letting me adjust, before he moves faster. The way he feels without the condom is pure bliss.

He moves faster and faster. My legs are shaking at this point, on the verge of giving out. His hand slides up my back before gripping my hair, and as he pulls, I arch my back. He hits a different angle. I freeze, and his other hand reaches under me and strokes my clit. My arms give out, and I fall face forward on the bed. I scream into my pillow, and he pounds harder, prolonging my orgasms, before he spills himself inside me.

He gently lies down on my back, and I let out a deep breath, trying to regain control of my shaking body. He kisses my shoulder, his breathing just as labored as mine. I think he attempted to kill me in that moment.

"You alive?" he asks, smoothing my hair over my shoulder.

"No." I say, my voice muffled by the pillow. He laughs, his body shaking against my back.

"Momma, you're beautiful."

"Sorry, I can't answer you. I'm dead." I close my eyes, just wanting sleep.

He laughs again. "I didn't know the dead could speak." He pinches my butt but I don't make a sound. "Oh is that how it's going to go?" he taunts. He gently slides out of me and picks me up off the bed. I stay completely limber.

He turns on the shower and immediately steps inside, the cold water hitting my back. I squeal and he laughs, turning around so the spray is hitting his back. I lock my legs around his waist.

"That was just mean." I pout, and he kisses my puckered lip.

"Poor baby."

I mock glare at him and he throws his head back, laughing at me. "You're beautiful." He kisses me, and I kiss him back because that is just something I can't control. The water is now warm, steam filling the bathroom.

"I bet you're exhausted." I can see it on his face.

His expression softens. "I am fine, baby. Today has been long, and we have to deal with the trafficking again. This is not the first time, and it won't be the last."

I shake my head in disbelief. "I know things like this are real and it happens every day, but to actually see it?" I close my eyes, thinking of Reid.

"It's fucking sick and we have to stop it. Justice doesn't always come from the police."

I open my eyes and look at him for a moment. "That is sometimes the best thing that can happen."

"Come on, baby. Let's get cleaned up and get in bed. Gabby will be up early."

I sigh. That is so true. The moment the light is shining through her window, she is up and at it. "She has gymnastics tomorrow morning." I totally forgot about it until this moment.

"We will take her together." He sets me down. I love that he wants to be there for the little things. That means a lot, and I know that is everything to Gabby.

The Next Morning

I turn over and look at the clock; it reads seven o'clock. I slide out of bed and put on a pair of Travis's sweats. Time to start breakfast and get her stuff ready for gymnastics. She learned the basics at her gym in Hawaii,

She loves it. She comes alive the moment she steps foot into that gym, and I want her to experience everything she loves. I want to give her the opportunity to live her dreams.

I put on a single breakfast of eggs, bacon, and some toast. I look at the clock, and we need to leave in an hour. When I walk up the stairs to wake her up, I look in my and Travis's room—he's not there.

In Gabby's room Travis is lifting her out of bed, her face tucked into the side of his neck. "Someone's sleepy, Momma," Travis whispers, rocking side to side. I smile at both of them, savoring this beautiful moment.

"What's for breakfast?" I can barely hear her voice. Travis gives me a look that says *how cute is she?* She really is the most adorable child ever.

"Bacon."

Her head whips around and she looks at me. "Bacon?" Her tiredness is gone in a split second. I nod and she wiggles, wanting down.

"Go sit at the table, sweetheart," I say as she runs off.

Travis laughs, "She is precious, Momma."

I nod. "She really is! Should we ask Aiden if he wants any breakfast?"

Travis knocks lightly on his door before opening it. "You want any breakfast?"

"I will be down in a few," Aiden says, his voice lighter from sleep.

We arrive at the gym. Gabby looks so cute in her little leotard. I have her hair plaited in two braids.

We are sitting in the parents' room, which has a large window so we can watch her run around on the mats. The coach bends down to tell her something, and she takes off, doing a front flip–at five years old! The coach's eyes light up. I want to run out of the room screaming, I am so proud of her. Travis is standing up looking out the window. "She is amazing."

The other mothers are staring at both of us. Travis is the only guy in this room full of women.

Even with the little training she's had, Gabby is already better than the other kids her age. She's always practiced, even outside the gym. I bought a mat for our living room, took out all the furniture, and let her practice as much as she wanted. She is a fast learner, and she won't stop until it's perfected.

"I will be back," Travis says. He kisses the top of my head and walks into the bathroom. One by one, all the women scoot close to me. "Girl, where can I find one of them?" one lady whispers, looking at the bathroom to make sure Travis doesn't hear. I laugh loudly at that. I don't blame her for asking.

"I didn't find him, he found me." I shrug. He took over my life the moment I met him. He dug his way in and stole my heart, then my baby's. From the moment I met him, he's been there for me and for her. Travis took on the role of Dad without even thinking about it. It's like it just came naturally to him.

"I hope one finds me!" One of the ladies smiles. "I'm Bailey."

The one closest to me raises her hand. "I'm Monica."

I smile at her. "It's nice to meet you, Monica."

The door opens and Travis walks in looking like sex on freaking stick; he is a walking sin. Monica sucks in a sharp breath. Oh honey, I understand completely. I have that same reaction to him on a daily basis. He sits down beside me, totally ignoring the other women.

Thirty minutes later the practice is over, and we all go into the gym. Gabby walks over, elated.

"Bailey, may I speak to you for a moment?" the coach asks, and I follow her over to the side of the gym.

Travis doesn't follow, but I take his hand and lead him with me. I want him to feel involved in everything. Gabby has run off to the mat to do more flips. She is just five but she is beyond her years.

"I never do this, but I wanted to see if you want to put your daughter into the elite group? It's a lot more hours and more money, but she will get further training." I look at Gabby, who is laughing as she plays with another kid, who is a few years older. "Your daughter is the best I have ever seen for her age. She is a lot better than some of the older kids, honestly. With some fine tuning, I do believe we have a future Olympian in our midst."

I let her words sink in, and I look at Travis and he nods at me. "Gabby, baby, come here." She runs over and I bend down. "The coach her wants to ask you something, it's up to you." I smile at the coach and, when she smiles back, I can see the excitement. She bends down and asks my daughter, and Gabby screams, jumping up and down. "Yes!" Then she stops and looks at me. "Is that okay, Mommy?"

"That is perfectly fine, angel."

She smiles that bright, beautiful smile and jumps up and down with pure happiness.

"Follow me," the coach says, "we need to sign some papers." I follow her and this time Travis doesn't hesitate. We sit down and my eyes widen at the price of everything. It's a lot but it will let Gabby do what she loves. Before I can take out my checkbook, Travis is already writing the check. My eyes wide, I open my mouth to argue, but he leans over and whispers in my ear, "Angel, let me do this. You guys are mine, I take care of mine." That leaves me speechless, and I just fall more in love with him. He isn't afraid to tell me what he really thinks.

We walk out into the gym, and Gabby runs over to us and grabs Travis's hand. "Ravis, can we get a burger?" She looks up at him with those huge, beautiful eyes, and I watch him melt.

"Yes, baby."

I hide my smile. Travis takes my other hand and, like a family, we walk out together.

"One, two, three..." Travis calls from the kitchen while Gabby and I are running around the house trying to find a hiding place.

Aiden is on the couch, laughing, as Gabby and I duck behind the couch. She covers her mouth trying not to giggle. "Ready or not...here I come!" Travis calls. Gabby hides her face in her arm, and I can see her body shaking with laughter. I hear Travis walking through the living room, and I peek around just as he turns the corner.

"Come on, baby." I take her hand and pull her into the kitchen. I open the cabinet door and slide inside with

Gabby right in front of me, and I shut the door behind us. We sit for a while, waiting for Travis to find us.

"Where, oh where are my girls at?" He calls from what seems like the living room. A second later the cabinet door is open, and Travis's face comes into view. He grabs my hands and pulls me out, dragging me across the floor. I laugh hysterically, and Travis starts tickling my sides.

"I am going to save you, Mommy!" Gabby screams and tackles Travis's side. He pretends to fall down sideways, and she lands on top of him and tickles him. "Now who's boss, huh?" Aiden and I laugh, and her little face is scrunched up, pretending to be tough.

"You think you're mean?" Travis picks her up and throws her up in the air. She laughs, her arms and legs flailing. He sets her down and she lies on his chest, still giggling.

"You're the best, Ravis."

She yawns and I look at the clock. It's around 2:00 p.m. "Want to take a nap, baby?" I brush her hair over her shoulder. She nods and I stand up, helping her up with me. "Go change into some comfy clothes, I will be up in a few." She runs up the stairs.

"What do you say we take a nap too?" Travis winks, letting me know we would be doing anything but sleeping. I hear my phone ringing from the living room, and I grab it off the coffee table and answer it without looking.

"Miss Cowell?" A man's voice says before I can even say hello.

"Yes, this is she."

"This is Mr. Downey, your father's lawyer. I am sorry to inform you of the passing of your father. You are needed here to discuss the will."

"What?" I sit down on the couch, shock riding through me. My father is dead, and I didn't even know it? My mother never even thought to tell me. I had hoped someday that we would be able to move forward and have a relationship. That is naive thinking, honestly, but every girl wants her father to be in her life and protect her.

"How soon can you get here?" he asks without emotion.

"I can be there tomorrow," I whisper, my voice cracking. Even though my father was shitty, he was still my father and I wanted him to be a dad.

"Call me when you land and we can schedule a time." He hangs up and I put down my phone without looking at anyone. I know if I look at Travis I won't be able to hold it in.

Gabby is lying in her bed and looking at the door, waiting for me. I pull the blanket up and kiss her forehead. I will never understand how a parent could not be in their kid's life, love them, and cherish them. "Sleep well, my baby."

She closes her eyes and I pull the door shut, just leaving it cracked. I slip into my bedroom, where Travis is already waiting for me. I shut the door and the first tear escapes. "Come to me, Momma." He opens his arms and I all but run to him, wanting him to take all of this away. I wish with everything in me to do it all over again. My biggest wish in life was to have a dad. I wanted someone to be there with me through thick and thin, hold my hand, and push me to be the best person I could be. "What happened?" He kisses my temple before stepping back to look at me. His thumbs catch my tears, wiping them away.

"My father passed away," I get out through a jumble of sobs and a ton of emotions that I can't even comprehend. He closes his eyes and pulls me into his lap, just holding me while I let out all the pain that I have suffered through the years. "My father died. Apparently, it was a quite a while ago, because that was my lawyer telling me that I need to be there for the reading of the will, which I don't understand because he hated me." Travis jumps. I look at him, wondering what is wrong.

"Your father hated you?" I can see he is pissed off.

I sigh, closing my eyes, before I get ready to unload everything. "My father and mother were just bad parents. They never raised me. That was left up to the nannies." I sniff, wiping my cheeks with the back of my hand. "I wanted nothing more than to have my parents in my life. But they never showed me any love, and I went to look for it in all the wrong places. That's where Randall came into the picture. My parents loved him until I got pregnant. When they found out I was pregnant with Gabby, they threw some clothes in a bag and gave me a hundred dollars. I can still see the look in his eyes when he threw my bag on the porch: a look of pure disgust. He told me that I was not his daughter. I was dead to him. I had nightmares for a year after that.

"I would never, ever do anything like that to Gabby. I would support her and be there with her every step of the way. It was so hard, I had no one. I had Gabby by myself. I did everything myself and did whatever I could to be the best mother I could be. I didn't care if I didn't eat for days. The smile on my baby's face gave me so much more."

Travis is shaking, and his fists are clenched at his sides. I open his hand. "I loved my family nonetheless. I just regret that I never got a chance to make it better."

"That is the worst fucking thing I have ever heard, baby." He shakes his head, his jaw clenched. "The thought of you suffering one second…" He trails off.

I lay my head on his chest. "That part of my life is over, Travis."

He looks me straight in the eye. "That shit will never fucking happen again. I have you, baby. I will always have you, always." He kisses me, tears rolling down my cheeks and mixing into our kiss. He breaks the kiss. "I will charter the plane for us tonight, and I will be with you every second of the way." That takes a huge load off my shoulders. I don't think I could face my family alone after all these years and after everything that happened. That pain is raw, even now.

"Sleep, angel," Travis says.

I close my eyes. So many thoughts are circulating through my brain, and my heart just hurts. It's also filled with dread about what is to come.

 ten

Bailey

We arrived in Hawaii early in the morning. Then we went straight to the hotel and had a long nap.

Travis had planned and booked everything for us, I didn't have to worry about a single thing. He even got us a suite so Gabby could have her own room. Now I am standing outside the lawyer's office, with Travis by my side and Gabby holding my hand. I am scared. I am about to see some people that I have not seen in over five years, the very people who treated me like I was trash and don't claim my angel. This is hard.

"You have this, Momma. Head up high and show them the person you are," he whispers in my ear. I kiss his cheek; then I straighten my shoulders, lift my chin, and walk up the steps. I know I look absolutely amazing. When I said he planned everything, I didn't mention that he bought me an amazing dress and shoes. I look like a million bucks. He is in a freaking suit, and my mouth has been dripping ever since he walked out of the bathroom. Gabby is wearing a green dress that shows off her beautiful brown hair.

When Travis opens the door and I step into the waiting room, eyes immediately go to me. Then my mom, my cousins, and my aunts look at Travis and eventually settle on Gabby, who is hiding behind his legs.

My mother stands up like she is about to take a step in my direction. I arch an eyebrow, daring her to do such a thing. The lawyer steps out of his office and looks at me, his eyes moving from my head to my toes. Travis wraps his arm around me and I smirk. I love his protectiveness.

They all file into the office, and I squeeze Travis's hand. He sits down right outside the office door. "Right here, Momma."

I smile and step inside, shutting the door behind me. I sit down on the chair closest to the door, and the lawyer waits for everyone to get situated before he starts. "I only called two of you here today, I guess you are here for moral support?" he asks the gang of people with my mom.

"We assumed that we were included in the will," one of my aunts says. I hate her. She has always been such a bitch.

"I am sorry, ma'am, but only two people are in this will."

One of my cousins gapes at the lawyer in disbelief. "You mean to tell me that he left her something?" She looks in my direction.

The lawyer looks confused. "Shall we get started? A year ago he revised his will." My mother looks shocked and, honestly, why would he change it? I never thought that I would be left anything. He probably just wanted a mockery to be made out of me. The lawyer takes out a letter. "He wanted me to read this out loud, but it is addressed to you, Bailey."

Dear Bailey,

You are the biggest regret I have in my life. I regret that way I treated you, and I will live with that for the rest of my life. I allowed myself to be manipulated, to be controlled, and that led to your not being a part of my life as you should have been. My wife's jealousy, hatred, and bitterness filled my every pore, and it changed me.

I tried to reach out, to apologize, and my wife told me that you died in childbirth. I was devastated. I thought you had died thinking that I didn't love you. That is not the case, but I was foolish, selfish and, honestly, just dumb. I hate myself for the way I have treated you, and I regret that I never got you meet your daughter. My grandchild.

Then I learned that your mother had lied. You were alive. It was too late, the damage was done, but I wanted to do something that I should have done in the beginning. I should have taken care of you. This is nothing, but it is all I have to give you and Gabby. I love you, I am sorry, and I will rest easy knowing you will forever be taken care of. I hope you can forgive me.

Love,
your dad.

The lawyer puts the letter down, and I stare at the wall above his head in pure disbelief. This is something I never expected. I know people can change; I just never expected it here. This has given me more than I will ever need, and I have peace in my heart knowing that, deep down, he did love me. He just didn't know how to show it.

No one is perfect. I will forgive him, and I hope he rests easy. He has the peace it seems he has been lacking for a long time.

I look at my mom, who told my father I was dead, and she doesn't even dare to look at me.

"Let's get to the reading of the will." The lawyer starts reading, and I sink further into my mind. "Bailey is to receive six hundred million dollars." My mouth opens. "Three hundred million dollars will be divided among her children, to be received when they are twenty-one years old." I cover my mouth. I can't believe this is happening. "Janet will receive a check of three thousand dollars a month for the rest of her life." What the fuck? My mother is completely pale, and her sisters and nieces are looking from her to me with panic. "Your husband has left you a letter, Janet." The lawyer starts reading.

Janet,

I know you're confused and angry at the amount of money I have given you. You have never once in your life gone without anything, unlike our daughter. We threw her a bag and a hundred dollars, wishing her well. I will forever regret that, but you will never be sorry.

I am leaving you more than she had. You will have your house and your cars, and the bills will be forever paid, but three thousand a month is all you will get. Oh, and before you start to contest it, you signed a prenup. I could have left you with nothing, but I am trying to turn over a new leaf and not be so cruel.

Have a good life, and good luck to your new husband, who I know you will be searching for the second you leave the lawyer's office.

Holy fuck, he just roasted the hell out of her. My mother looks at me for the first time since she stepped inside the office. She was smug then, but now? Not so much.

"Mrs. Cowell, I will start your payments immediately. I will be back in touch. I need to speak with Bailey here. We have things to go over." My mother's face is completely red at being dismissed like that. Her sisters tear her out of the room, and she slams the door shut.

"Would you like me to wire the funds into your account?"

Travis

I have been staring at the fucking door ever since Bailey stepped inside. I want to tear that door off the hinges just to make sure she is okay. I hope that they didn't just bring her here to humiliate her; she has been through more than enough.

Gabby is playing on my phone, leaning into my side. "Ravis, when will Mommy be out?" she asks just as the door is wrenched open.

Bailey's mom and the other ladies step out looking pissed. I know that she is Bailey's mom, because Bailey looks a lot like her. "I can't believe this!" she screams and runs out of the building. That is not what I expected one bit. Almost an hour later Bailey walks out in a daze. She takes my hand and leads me out of the building to our car.

She stares out the window before looking at me and laughing, and she hands me a letter. I read it and I am shocked too. I am so fucking happy for her. This has to give her a bit of peace. "He left me everything. Six hundred million dollars and three hundred million to be divided among Gabby and our future kids. I never fucking expected that." She bends over at the waist and laughs uncontrollably. "He left my mother three thousand a month for the rest of her life."

I laugh because that is fucking amazing. That woman told Bailey's father she is dead, and she doesn't deserve an ounce of sympathy.

"I may have money, but it doesn't change a thing in my eyes. I won't allow it to change me," she tells me.

"I have money too, baby. Maybe not six hundred million, but you would never want for anything—vacations every week if you wanted."

She smiles. "I know what I want to do." She turns around in her seat and faces me. "I want to open a place, like a huge house... It's going to be a place for mothers, like me, who struggle to get on their feet. We will set them up with jobs, transportation—everything needed to give them a leg up in life. I will put the rest away for our kids."

She said *our kids* once again, hitting me right in my fucking soul. I touch the side of her face. "I think that is a beautiful idea, baby."

She smiles, and I want to tell her so fucking bad, right now, that I love her. "I love you, Momma, I can't fucking hold it in anymore. I know it's soon but none of that matters."

"I love you too, Travis, so much." She kisses me, and I bury my hands in her hair, kissing her back hard.

"YAY! About time!" Gabby cheers from the back seat, and we both pull back laughing.

"I love you too, baby." I tell Gabby, and her grin widens.

"I know it, Ravis, you tell me every day. I love you too." My poor fucking heart. This is the life, this is everything.

"I say we go to the beach, what do you guys think?" I say.

Gabby gasps dramatically. "Can we please?" He laughs. "Let's get to the hotel and change."

Bailey

Travis and I are under an umbrella watching Gabby play in the sand a few feet in front of us. I feel at peace. One part of me doesn't want to take that money, but Gabby deserves to have everything in life. I can put her through college. Hell, I can put all of my kids through college. Plus I can open a center for teen moms, so they won't have to struggle the way I did. It gives me major relief that Gabby will never know what it's like to go hungry and she has an amazing future.

"What has you thinking so hard?" Travis asks. He is absolutely beautiful in his swimming trunks. His abs, the tattoos going down his arms and sides. Every single woman on this beach has turned her full attention to Travis, and I don't blame them one bit.

"Can we go swim?" Gabby looks up at us.

"Let's go." I stand up, brushing the sand off my legs. Travis takes her little hand and mine, and we walk down to the water. I bend down, splashing water on both of them.

Gabby gasps. "Momma," she scolds and I laugh. She puts her fist on her hip. "Let's get her, Ravis!"

I take off running, laughing at the sight of her determined little face. An arm bands around my waist, and

Travis throws me out into the water and I land with a splash. I stand up, my hair in my face, and Gabby laughs. "You're a drowned rat." I push my hair out of my face, glaring at her.

Travis picks her up and throws her in right next to me. She stands up and gives him the stink eye. "Let's get him, Momma." She grabs my hand, and together we run after him. Both of us tackle his side, and we all fall into the water. When we come up, Travis is holding Gabby and we all laugh together.

I notice the looks all around us. What are they thinking? Then it hits me that we look like a family.

"Is my little mermaid thirsty?" Travis asks Gabby.

"A lemonade would be nice." I snort at the proper voice that she just attempted.

Travis hands her off to me. "What do you want, Momma?" His hand is on my ass. I arch my eyebrows at him, smirking. He is an ass man and, luckily for him, all of my baby weight went straight down there.

"Lemonade is good for me too."

He walks up the beach to a place where they sell snacks and drinks. "Want to sit down?" She nods and I set her down beside me, the waves hitting our lower half. "Do you miss living here?"

"No, I like Texas better. Ravis is in Texas." She finds a seashell and turns it over, admiring it.

"I love Texas too, angel."

A few minutes later Travis comes back and sits down beside me before handing us our drinks. I lean against his shoulder, and he kisses the side of my head.

"I really do love you." I lift my head and look at him, and he cups my face in his hands.

"And I really love you, Momma." He kisses me, and I smile against his lips, my hand on top of his on my cheek. He pulls back and starts spreading kisses all over my face. I laugh, trying to swat him away.

"Ravis." Gabby burrows her way between us, and she looks scared. She points down the beach, and I see my mother standing there with two guys. She is pointing at the three of us. My mouth dries.

"Baby, take Gabby and get to the truck." His voice is different than the way he usually talks to us. This is badass biker Travis speaking.

I stand up with her in my arms, bend down to grab the keys and my phone, and run up the beach. Travis follows us, and I see a glint of metal before he sticks it in the back of his shorts. He walks to the bathroom; I guess he wants to be away from the view of others. I am shaking so much I can barely hold Gabby up. I put her in the car. "Get in your seat, baby," I tell her. She scrambles to the back and I lock the door.

A man bangs on our window. My breath stills and terror rides through my body. I don't want Gabby to see this. I can kick some ass when needed, but I am not invincible, and it's not easy to take down a man, especially one that size. I scoot into the driver's side of the truck and put it in drive. I back out of there, not even waiting to see if he gets out of the way. I drive toward the bathroom to see if Travis needs to make a run for it.

Travis

How fucking dare these idiotic shitheads try to stir up shit in front of my daughter?

I stand at the entrance to the bathroom waiting on these fuckers to step inside so I can give them an ass whooping.

Bailey's fucking mother walks into the bathroom first, a huge smirk on her face like she won something. "I am sure my daughter will hand over all of the money once we kill you, then try to kill Gabby." Then the men with her step inside, hitting Janet with the door. She falls to the floor. They look down at her for a moment then come at me. I duck and punch. I kick and elbow. I fucking beat the ever-living shit out of them until they are knocked out on the ground next to her. All of this happens in three minutes.

Janet groans, holding her head, and I bend down so I am face-to-face with her. Her eyes widen. "Listen here, bitch, I don't give a fuck if you want your money—you are not getting shit. I am with the Grim Sinners MC, and do you want war with the whole club?" Her eyes widen again at the name of my MC; we are known worldwide for a fucking good reason. We don't play. "Good, you get it.

This is your only fucking warning." I stand up. She nods and I walk out of the bathroom.

My first thought is *why is Bailey here?* Then I see the fucker running down the road toward them. I open the driver's side door of the truck. Bailey scoots over to the passenger seat, and her face is pale with fear and adrenaline. Gabby doesn't fully understand what is happening, thank goodness. "Does ordering some pizza at the hotel sound good to you, angel baby?" I ask her.

She smiles. "Can we watch movies too, Ravis?"

The fucker is still running toward us, so I turn the truck around and drive right toward him. I swerve to the side at the last second and open my door. He slams into it and falls to the ground rolling. Then the truck jumps like I hit a pothole. I look back and see him holding his leg. "Damn pothole," I say out loud.

"That's a bad word, Ravis." Gabby giggles.

I grab Bailey's hand, and I pull her over to the middle seat next to me. "Are you okay, Momma?"

She nods, laying her head on my shoulder. "I am okay, I am glad you're okay. What happened?" she whispers so Gabby doesn't hear.

"Your mom hired these guys to convince you to give her the money."

"I don't understand how people are like this. I just want to go home."

I can tell she is deeply saddened by everything, and I can say I don't blame her. Her mother hired someone to scare and possibly hurt her on top of threatening Gabby, but I don't want her to know that. She has already been through so fucking much, so much. She needs to live her life peacefully without worrying about shit like this happening.

"Want to head home tomorrow?" I ask Gabby, looking in the rearview mirror.

"Yes! I miss baby Reid and Aiden."

I laugh. I will have to tell Aiden. "Whatever my girls want." I wink at Gabby in the mirror, and she giggles.

eleven

A Month and a Half Later

I wake up, and the first thing that hits me is that I have not started my period. From the moment Travis and I got home from Hawaii, we have been like rabbits.

You won't hear a complaint from me. But I cover my face, kind of afraid of what the outcome will be. I want to be a mom—don't get me wrong—but it's also scary that I will be doing it all over again.

I look at the clock on the nightstand. It's ten o'clock in the morning. Travis left thirty minutes ago to take Gabby to practice. It's literally just ten minutes from our house, so he will be back soon. I sit on the edge of the bed and rub my eyes.

I hear the door open downstairs, and my heart starts pounding. Do I tell him of my suspicion? Thump, thump, thump. I hear him walk up the stairs, and it's grating on my nerves more and more by the second. He steps into the room looking way too fucking delicious. He is wearing a tight black shirt under his vest and light blue jeans. He looks into my eyes, and I suck in a sharp breath. He still takes my breath away.

We haven't really been apart since the moment we met, and I couldn't imagine it being any different. Life is just perfect with him around—he has completed our life. He steps further into the room. I feel like something is wrong." I can hear the hesitancy in his voice.

I shake my head. "Nothing is wrong, I just realized something." My hands are shaking, and my insides are quivering right along with it. I am afraid of his reaction. Of course it's been planned, but that doesn't mean old habits don't die hard. "I haven't had my period."

His eyes widen and he looks at my stomach. "You mean there could be…"

I laugh, the worry completely gone. "Yes, we need to get a pregnancy test to be sure."

He puts a finger up. "I have some." I watch in shock as he opens a drawer in his bedside table and takes out a couple tests. "When did you get those?" I whisper yell, feeling even more foolish for my reaction. He shrugs. "Kind of ever since we decided to try for a baby."

I take the box, and we walk together to the bathroom. I place my hand on his chest. "Wait here." He twists his lips, and I know he wants to argue. "Baby, you're not watching me pee." He rolls his eyes and sits on the bed. He looks so cute pouting. I shut the door and walk to the toilet.

I pee on the sticks and now we wait. I open the bathroom door and he practically runs inside. He is so cute. I'm starting to get excited. I would love to see him holding our baby. He is so good with Gabby. She loves him, and she has him totally wrapped around her little finger. I catch him daily playing dress-up with her and letting her put makeup on him. He doesn't care. He will walk around the house with pink eye shadow and it doesn't faze him. That is a good fucking man.

She wanted a top that had dinosaurs, but it was labeled as a boys' shirt. She started to put it back, but he told her she can dress however she wants and be whatever she wants to be in life. I wanted to jump his bones on sight, and she grabbed the shirt and hugged it to her chest.

"This wait is fucking killing me." Travis paces the bathroom, and I grab the belt loop of his jeans as he walks past.

"Give me some smooches, baby." I pooch my lips out dramatically. He rolls his eyes and kisses me; then he plants kisses all over my face. I bend down trying to escape the onslaught, and he picks me up, nipping at my neck.

"We better check the test," I manage to get out through my heavy laughter, and he lets me go so fast I almost lose my balance. He grabs the test and stares at it. It's a digital one that flat-out tells you if you're pregnant or not. "Travis?" I ask. He doesn't have any expression on his face.

"Momma," he says, and I peek over and see it. A big, bold word: *pregnant*.

I cover my mouth, tears pooling in my eyes. "I'm pregnant."

He puts the test down on the counter, bends down, and kisses me with so much passion. I grip his shirt, kissing him back with everything in me. He pulls away and kisses my forehead before resting his forehead against mine. I feel him shaking. "We are having a baby," he says.

All of a sudden he falls to his knees, scaring me. He pulls my shirt, pressing a kiss directly below my navel. I tilt my head back, so emotional, so overwhelmed. "Hey baby, Daddy can't wait to meet you," he says, rubbing my sides.

My heart has been shattered into a million pieces—he so sweet and caring and just so kind. I finally look down at him, and he has an expression of pure bliss. He looks up at me, grinning. "Gabby is going to be a big sister, she will be such a good fucking big sister."

I cup his face in my hands. "She will, and you will be an amazing dad." I bend down and kiss the top of his head.

"Wait, are you sure you're supposed to bend?" He stands and picks me up. *Let the panicking begin.*

"Travis, bending over isn't going to hurt me."

He shakes his head. "I am not taking a fucking chance." He is dead serious. I snort and bury my head in his chest, laughing. I think this is going to be a long couple of months.

"Now I need to give my momma some lovin's." He pinches my ass.

"I heard that sex was bad for the baby."

His face pales, then gets even paler. "But we have been having sex, we need to get you to the hospital." He looks genuinely scared.

"I was just joking." I laugh.

He leans back against the counter. "Don't do that shit to me. I can't handle things like that."

"I am sorry, baby." My phone starts ringing, and I walk out of the bathroom to answer it.

"Hello?" I hear nothing over the line. "Hello?" I hang up and look at the caller ID; it says *unknown caller* once again. For the past week I have been getting weird calls like this.

"Who was that?" Travis asks. I finally tell him about the weird calls I've been getting for the past week.

"What the fuck, why haven't you told me?"

I shrug. "I honestly just thought it was a telemarketer or something."

He wraps his arm around me and takes out his phone. "I am texting our tech guy and having him trace the calls." I hand him my phone and let him deal with that.

"I also need to find a baby doctor. I need to be seen."

"Go cuddle up on the couch, and I will book your appointment, Momma." He taps my ass.

"Don't rush me," I tease him but I just let him handle it for me. It's been just me for a long time, and it's nice to be able to sit on the couch, just relaxing. I turn back at the door. "Thank you, Travis. For being you and for everything you do for Gabby and me."

"I love you, baby. There's nothing I wouldn't do for you and Gabby."

"I love you too, baby."

Travis

"I hope it's a boy," Bailey tells me, looking down at her still-flat stomach, "I know Gabby has mentioned wanting a baby brother."

"I don't care, I just want him or her to be completely healthy." I place my hand on her belly. I can't wait until it is rounded and I can feel the baby inside. Then the day I get to hold my child.

"I wish that I met you years ago and you were Gabby's dad."

It fucking kills me that she went through everything she did. That she fed her daughter when she hadn't eaten in days. Her family was beyond fucking loaded, and she had absolutely nothing. That shit fucking kills me, right down to my soul.

But she did it. I'm so fucking proud of her. She held her shit together and did what the fuck she needed to do.

My phone rings and I look down to see it's our tech guy, Corey. A moment later I jump off the couch. "I am going there now." I run to the door.

"What the hell is happening?" Bailey says. She is pale.

"He traced the call and it was from outside Gabby's gym." I don't want to worry her, but she needs to know. "I am going there right now. Press this button here when I leave, and the house will be completely locked down until I am back." I point to the button and she nods, her arms across her chest.

"I want to go with you."

"She is fine, baby. I will call you the second I have my eyes on her. I just want to make sure everything is okay."

Bailey

The wait for them to get home is pure agony.

Although it went against everything in me, I understand why he wanted me to stay here. He will make sure she is safe—I know that right down to my soul.

He finally calls to let me know he has eyes on her and everything is okay. So I stand in front of the window, waiting for them to pull up in the driveway. I still don't know what happened. Maybe it's my mom trying to pull something?

His truck turns into the driveway. I go to the security panel and unalarm everything and run out onto the porch. I am shaking. I just want to hold my baby.

Travis gets out and flashes me a smile, trying to make me feel better. He walks over to Gabby's side of the vehicle, and I see her little feet hit the ground. She runs to me, and I bend down and pick her up, hugging her tightly. "I missed you, angel baby!" I squeeze her, rocking her gently from side to side.

She giggles. "I missed you too, Momma." She pats my back, like a grown up.

"What do you want for lunch?" I put her down and hold her hand.

"A nap?"

I laugh because that is something not many kids want to do. My daughter has always loved her sleep. "I think that can be arranged, but I need to feed you first." I open the door and she steps inside the house and runs to her toys in the corner of the room. Travis hugs me to his chest. I close my eyes and breathe in his scent, letting every single worry go. She is here, she is safe, and I am here with Travis.

"We have an appointment with the doctor tomorrow." He gently massages my back, trying to loosen my tense muscles. I look up smiling, remembering that I am pregnant. "Sounds good, I love how you said *we*."

"We are in this together, for everything."

I am so blessed. I am so blessed with everything that has happened in my life, starting with my daughter.

"Tonight we are having a family barbecue at the club, want to go?"

I think on it for a split second. I would be meeting everyone in the club, which is practically his family. "I would love to."

"Good, they are going to love you and Gabby."

Bailey

I am sitting on the couch, waiting until it's time to go to the club, and Travis sets a box in my lap.

"What is this?"

He waves his hand. "You have to open it." I lift the lid and push back the paper, and then I see it. There's a cut with a patch on the back, saying *Property of Travis*. I look at him in pure shock. This is big deal in the MC world. I mean *huge*, because this is his way of telling the world I am his. This is like marriage in their world, and he is giving it to me. "Is this what I think it is?" My hands shake as I touch the part of the patch that says *Travis*.

"Yes, it's yours." He is on his knees in front of me, watching my reaction.

"Want to put it on me?" I take the vest out of the box. He takes it from me and I turn around, putting my arms through the holes. I close my eyes and it's really real.

"You look fucking amazing," he growls in my ear, grabbing my ass. I turn around and kiss him, both of my hands gripping his shirt. This is a moment I will never forget, another huge step in our lives together. I kiss his cheek. Then I rest my forehead against his chin as a song comes over the radio. He gathers me more tightly in his arms, until my toes are on top of his. He takes my breath away as he slow dances with me right there in the living room.

I feel a hand on my leg. Gabby is standing next to us. Travis bends down and picks her up, and we all dance together. This is something that I hope Gabby will remember when she is older. One day she is going to fall in love, and I want her to fall in love with someone who will treat her the way he treats me. I want her to have the best in life. I don't want her to know the struggles I have had.

Once the song is over, I step off his toes.

"I got you something too, Gabby." He sets her down on the couch and hands her a box that is a bit smaller than mine.

"Thank you, Ravis," she says before she opens it. My daughter would be happy to accept a banana. She opens the lid and pushes back the paper. It's a little vest just for her, and it says: *Travis's baby girl.* Oh my goodness. I shake my head in disbelief at how amazingly perfect he is. I know that I am repeating this over and over, but it's true.

"Oh Ravis, I love it! We will be matching." She jumps off the couch holding the vest, and she puts it on before either of us can help her. She claps her hands together, spins in a circle, and grins at both of us.

"You look beautiful, baby."

She flips her hair over her shoulder. "I know."

I snort and burst out laughing. I love her confidence. Travis shakes his head, grinning, before grabbing his keys off the coffee table. "You guys ready to go?"

"I'm ready."

Gabby jumps up and down. "Me too! Will there be kids to play with?"

Travis pulls at one of her curls. "Yes, there are a bunch of littles."

I'm kind of in awe of the huge difference I see in her. When we first arrived, she was so scared of everyone she hid behind my legs, but she was never scared of Travis. She took to him immediately, and he did the same with her. Travis and Gabby established an amazing relationship before he and I did. He was a father to her from the start.

We get to the clubhouse and pull around to the back. There are quite a few people and a bunch of motorcycles all over the property.

I see Adeline and Smiley and Wilder and Joslyn, and I immediately feel better. Lane is here too, and I meet his wife and their daughter, Tiffany. Some of the members of the Devil Souls MC are also here today. Aiden comes out of the large building holding baby Reid. My hands are immediately itching to hold him.

Travis sets Gabby down, and she takes off screaming, "Baby Reid!" Everyone's attention turns to Gabby then to us. Adeline smiles and waves, motioning us over. Travis's hand is at the small of my back, leading me to everyone. They all have smiles on their faces, making me feel welcome.

This is his family. What if they don't like me? What would that do to Travis? I close my eyes, trying not to let the insecurities in. *You've been doing so amazing with your anxiety, no need to backtrack.*

We approach Smiley and Adeline. Smiley is holding baby Noah and Remy in his arms. Adeline steps forward and hugs me. "So glad to see you!" She takes Noah from Smiley.

I have to take a second to admire Smiley. He has aged well. I don't mean to look at another man, because Travis is the hottest thing ever, but Smiley is totally hot too, with that silver fox thing going on. Smiley smirks at me like he knows what I am thinking. I feel my face getting hot, and I turn around to check on Gabby, who is sitting in a chair next to Aiden, holding Reid.

Travis takes me over to Lane, and I smile at the woman standing next to him. She is very beautiful. "Nice to meet you, I'm Amelia."

"It's nice to meet you too." I smile at her and she returns it. It's a real smile, something that no one in my family possesses. I wish so much that I had a family like he has. I know most them aren't blood, but the bonds of love and loyalty are there. Blood isn't always thicker than water. Oil and rubber are a bit stronger than all of that.

"Tomorrow night we are having a girls' night. The ole ladies from both MCs are getting together for a night of fun," Amelia says.

"Go, baby. I will watch Gabby. We can go have a night out ourselves, food and maybe a movie."

Amelia grins ear-to-ear, making me feel like I am going to be in all kinds of trouble. "We will be by to pick you up at eight."

"My poor ovaries!" a lady says, and I turn around to see an ole lady in the Devils dramatically fanning her face, looking at Aiden holding his son. A man walks up to her, whispers in her ear, and grins wickedly. I laugh under my breath. I need to be her friend.

I decide to take the initiative, so I walk over to her. "Hey, I'm Bailey."

She grins at me, and I can tell right away that she is major trouble. "I'm Jean and this hunk of hotness is my baby daddy." Smack! She doesn't even jump; she pretends that he just didn't smack her on the ass. I laugh at their playfulness.

"Are you up to no good again?" A woman with eyes like Lane's and Smiley's walks up. I know that this is Smiley's daughter, Shaylin, the Grim Sinners princess. He used to be the president of the Grim Sinners, before he handed the role to Lane. Most of the older members have retired. They are still around, of course, but they have let the younger generation take over.

"I am always up to no good," she says, and her man sighs and walks away. She laughs. "It's so easy to get him riled up."

Shaylin rolls her eyes. "We all know, Jean." She looks at me. "Bailey?"

I nod, smiling. "That's me."

"It's very nice to meet you."

"It's nice to meet you too!"

"You going to the girls' night?" she asks me.

"Yes! I will be there." I am excited. I have never had a proper girls' night. Having a baby at eighteen years old changed a lot of things for me. She is my life, and that is something I will never regret. I do wish it could have been different though.

"Let the men babysit and raise hell," Jean gloats, looking back at her man, who completely ignores her. She turns around, sighing. "I do love him."

"Mommy!" Gabby is running in my direction with a ton of kids.

"Yes, baby?" I bend down to her level.

"Can I have a sleepover sometime and invite my friends?"

I look at the crowd of kids behind her and, without hesitation, I nod. She screams and starts bouncing around. "I just have to tell Ravis!" she says before taking off at a full sprint.

He bends down in a similar fashion and grins before winking at me. I put my hand over my heart. "Girl, you're one lucky bitch. He is beautiful, and the way he is with your baby is perfect," Jean says, and I agree with her wholeheartedly.

Adeline pops out of nowhere holding baby Reid. "All of our men are like this. We are all blessed."

"Can I?" I ask her and she hands Reid to me. I snuggle him and breathe in that baby smell. Travis's eyes darken as he watches me with Reid, and I know he is thinking of me and our future baby. Sometimes I forget, and then it just hits me that I really am pregnant. That I will have a baby, Travis's baby. That's a lot to take in. My life has changed so completely, but I don't want to think about it too much until I see the doctor tomorrow.

"You guys ready to eat?" someone yells and everyone starts making their way to a huge table filled to the brim with food. My mouth waters at the sight of ribs, steaks, and rolls. They have all the good stuff, and all of my manners are about to go out the window while I dive face first into the ribs. I have not had ribs in years, back when I was home with my parents, actually.

"Baby, come here."

Gabby runs over and I hand her a plate.

"Do you know what you want?"

She looks at the food. "Just a cheeseburger."

I reach over and grab a burger for her, and I set it on her plate with some fries. "Do you need me to help carry?"

She shakes her head. "I am going to go with my friends." She runs off, two fries slipping over the edge of her plate.

Travis is standing next to me, filling his plate with ribs. Our minds are on the same track. I grab half a rack of ribs; then I find a picnic table to park my butt on. Travis sits next to me, and he has twice the amount food that I do.

He sets down packets of wipes on the table. "You are the real MVP."

He smirks at me. "Baby, if you don't get dirty eating ribs, then you're not doing it right." I grab a rib and take a huge bite. I close my eyes and moan. I know I may look like an idiot, but I don't have it in me to care one bit. Travis and I bond over ribs. We don't speak, but we wipe the barbecue sauce off each other's faces; that is true love.

Later that evening, as daylight is waning, we spread out a blanket on the lawn for the fireworks. Aiden left because he didn't want the loud noises to scare Reid. Gabby is sitting in front of us with Tiana, Shaylin's little girl. They are pretty close in age. Gabby just turned five, and she is a year or two older. She is currently taking apart a toy car and showing Gabby how to put it back together.

"That's awesome! I'm good at flipping." Gabby, being her dramatic self, runs along the field and starts performing back flips. She is really amazing; it catches me off guard a lot of the time, honestly. She has scared me ever since she took the notion to start jumping off of things and flipping in midair. She runs back and plops her butt right down. "See!" She grins, so happy with herself.

"Good job!" Tiana says and I cover my mouth so I don't laugh. It's so funny to hear kids acting beyond their age.

I look at Shaylin, who is sitting next to me with her man, Butcher. He is huge, and he looks mean. It's so wild so see them together, because they are total opposites. I have heard rumors that she's just as vicious as he is. I sure

LeAnn Ashers

never want to find out. I do have a side of myself that has a major temper, but it's more a protective instinct.

The fireworks shoot up in the air, and I look up at the sky. Travis holds my hand and, as a family, we celebrate our first fourth of July together.

166

twelve

Bailey

We walk inside the bar and instantly start screaming as we see the Devil Souls girls. There are a few of them I haven't met yet.

Joslyn is sticking to my side, and I am very thankful because I'm still getting used to everyone. These ladies are so different from the women I am used to, who are catty and two-faced. They seem genuinely nice.

We all sit down at a huge round table in the back. It's big enough for everyone but small enough that everyone can talk to each other.

"Hi! To those who haven't met Bailey yet, she is Travis's old lady," Joslyn says.

I smile at the ones I haven't met. The lady closest to me speaks first. "My name is Kayla, I am the VP of the Devils Ladies." She smiles and leans back so I can see the next lady. I know who she is immediately. Her smile is like her mother's.

"Your mom is Adeline?" I ask before she can speak.

She laughs. "Yeah, that's my mom. Pretty great, isn't she?"

We all nod. "You're very lucky," I say. I would kill for my own mother to be like that.

"My name is Alisha, in case you didn't know."

"It's nice to meet you."

Then the only girl I haven't met, who is closer to my age than some of the others, speaks up. "I'm Paisley. I am Liam's old lady and Torch is my dad."

"It's nice to meet you all."

"SHOTS!" Jean screams and a few waiters hustle over. I cover my mouth so I don't laugh. The waiter goes around the table taking orders. I shake my head and ask for water. I notice all of the girls' eyes are on me. Uh oh.

Once the waiters leave, in sync, all the girls scoot closer to me. I lick my lips, trying to pretend that I don't notice.

"Uhh, girl," Jean says, her eyes narrowed on me with that mom look.

"Okay, I just found out yesterday that I am pregnant, but that's not one hundred percent certain because I am going to the doctor tomorrow." Much to my surprise they stand up, screaming, and run straight to me. Congrats are offered by everyone, along with hugs and belly touches. Such amazing women.

"Travis will be such an amazing dad." Joslyn grins at me. I know she and Travis are pretty close friends, because he and Wilder are close.

"He already is, he is so perfect with Gabby."

They all aww and I grin at their reactions. Jean sighs the loudest, putting her hand over her heart. "Nothing hotter than a biker being a dad." That is so true; it seems like all of these guys are great dads. They are very present and involved. I love that.

Randall was never really a dad. He is just a sucky individual. Until I met Travis I never realized how poorly I had been treated by him. I let way too much stuff go because it was just easier. That should never have happened.

All of the ladies talk about their jobs, kids, and whatever they want as the drinks are being passed around. "What do you want to do?" Kayla asks me. "Besides being a kick-ass mom. That's a job in itself."

I'm going to be opening a couple of homes for single mothers, especially teenagers. So they can have help being independent."

Joslyn hugs me. She knows this means a lot to me. I never want another soul to go hungry so her child can eat, the way I did. I was so desperate to get her some formula I went door to door asking if I could cut people's hair for just a few bucks. That hurt my pride so much, but that didn't matter when it came to my daughter.

"You were a single mother, weren't you?" Alisha asks me.

"Yes I was, my parents kicked me out once they found out I was pregnant. All I had was a small bag of clothes and one hundred dollars. It was very hard." I am not ashamed of my past. I survived and now I am thriving.

"So proud of you, girl." Amelia hugs me and I hug her back. This feels so amazing, just to talk and be myself with these girls.

"Thank you all so much."

"You guys ready to dance?" Jean slams her glass on the table and jumps to her feet, dragging Shaylin with her. We all laugh and follow her. Jean is buzzed already, but I think she started drinking before she even got here.

There are some MC guys stationed across the bar, discreetly watching out for us. I know the MC worries about keeping everyone safe first and foremost. Travis kind of explained to me that they and the Devils have made some enemies because they take down a lot of bad guys. Plus, although every girl here can handle herself—I know I can—going against grown men isn't the greatest idea.

I am standing back from everyone, keeping an eye out. They are throwing back shots left and right, loosening up and dancing. Jean is swaying around like the tall balloon man you see a lot at car dealerships. I laugh when she bends back so far and then snaps forward.

Joslyn is still close by. I feel very protective of her. She is so sweet and kind—I know she doesn't have a mean bone in her body. I feel like she has been through a lot, but she is always smiling. She's a very strong woman who has been dealt a shitty hand. She walks over to me. "I am going to the bathroom."

"I will come with." As we wade through all of the grinding bodies, I notice one of the MC guys and he nods. He has a prospect patch on.

As we take turns in the bathroom stall, I have a feeling something is not right. When I step out of the stall, Joslyn is standing in the corner, pushing away a man who is right in her face. First off, where the fuck is the prospect? Isn't this his job? Wait until I get a hold of that fucker!

I grab a beer bottle. "Hey, fucker." He turns around to face me. Eww, he is gross. He's wearing a stained white shirt and smells like he has taken a beer bath.

"Leave her alone." I tell him, my voice strong. She is shaking and that just makes me ten times angrier. He can tell that she doesn't want him to be all up in her face. Why the fuck do some people think it's okay to harass others?

Joslyn ducks out from behind him and starts in my direction, and he grabs her arm. She winces and I jump into action. I punch him in the face as hard as I can. I hear something crack in my hand, and I ignore the pain. He stumbles back, letting her go. I kick him in the stomach, and he falls back on his ass. Then I smash my beer bottle against his head, glass shattering everywhere. He hits the floor with a thump, his eyes rolling back in his head, knocked out.

Joslyn is staring at me with wide eyes. The other girls are standing behind her, grinning. Two of them are holding phones, probably taking a video. "Damn, girl. I didn't know you had a temper like that," Shaylin says.

I shrug. I don't lose my temper often, but I have momma bear branded into me.

"The guys are on their way," Amelia says.

"Ours are too," Kayla says.

Joslyn pales slightly. "I am sorry for ruining girls' night." It's comical the way everyone's head snaps in her direction at once.

"You didn't. I always love to see a good fight," Shaylin tells her.

Joslyn looks better. I try to take her hand, but I almost hit the ground at the pain. I look at my hand. It's completely swollen and already bruising.

Jean pops out of nowhere. "Oh damn, I think you've broken something."

Joslyn runs behind the bar and comes back, a second later, with a towel and ice.

"Thank you."

She holds her hand up. "No, you got hurt because of me."

I take her to the side. "Don't you dare feel guilty. You're my friend, and I wasn't going to let you be harassed by someone right in front of my face." With my good arm I wrap her in a hug, squeezing her slightly.

The door opens with a bang. Wilder runs in and Travis is right behind him, looking angry. Wilder touches Joslyn's face. "Baby, you okay?"

Travis looks at my hand and touches it gently. I wince, feeling sick to my stomach. "Fuck baby, we need to get you to the hospital. How did you do that?"

Jean comes out of nowhere again, holding a phone. "I know how!" She hands Travis the phone, and he and Wilder watch as, with one punch, I almost knock the guy on his ass. "Fuck, baby." Travis looks at my hand again.

Wilder pushes him out of the way and hugs me. "Thank you for protecting my wife."

"That's what family is for, right?"

He stares at me for a beat and nods, grinning. I hear a door open and then a "What the fuck?" It's the stupid prospect who was supposed to be watching us. I march over to him, and he looks at my hand and then at Travis, who is at my back. I start to throw a punch with my left hand. Travis catches my fist and does the job for me, punching him so hard in the face he hits the ground, knocked out.

"What the fuck, both of you are sluggers," Jean slurs and her man throws her over his shoulder and carries her out of there.

"Come on, we need to get you to the hospital." Travis puts his hand at the small of my back. I glare at the prospect lying on the ground. If he had been doing his job, none of this would have happened and girls' night would still be in full swing. The girls wave at me, smiling, as Travis leads me out of the bar, and I wave back with my good hand.

"Another night soon?" I ask them.

"Yes!" they all yell back and I laugh. I guess we are all trouble. I mean if we can handle being with bikers, how can we not be?

"Wait, where's Gabby?" I ask Travis.

"Aiden walked over to stay with her. She's in bed so I doubt she will even notice me gone."

"Good, she loves Aiden anyway." I follow him to his truck. "I'm disappointed that we aren't on your bike.".

"Don't pout. First, you're hurt and second, you're carrying precious cargo, Momma." He touches my stomach and opens my door, and my pouting is gone in that second. He helps me into the truck. I can't use my right hand, and that's put a damper on my climbing skills. He shuts the door, and I lean my head back against the headrest, closing my eyes. My hand is throbbing like a heartbeat.

He shuts his door. I look over at him and he is staring at me. "Hurting?"

I nod. I don't really want to speak at the moment. The adrenaline is wearing off, and the pain is really starting to sink in.

"I am fucking sorry, baby." He rubs my leg.

"I will be fine." I grin at him. Well, I try to.

Breaking your wrist is for the freaking birds. The x-ray was painful. The bone on the side of my wrist is cracked. I almost needed surgery to fix it but, luckily, I can get away with a cast.

I lay my head on Travis's shoulder while they put the cast on me. We made sure to tell the doctor that I may be pregnant before we did the x-ray. It's not the most fun thing ever being poked and prodded, but I'm not taking any kind of pain meds in case it would affect the baby. This is sucky, but I would never jeopardize him or her. I do hope it's a boy, a little boy who looks just like Travis.

An hour later we are leaving the hospital, and I am ready to go home and sleep. As we get in the truck, I rub my eyes, yawning. The clock in the truck reads 1:00 a.m. "Can you see how Joslyn is?" I ask.

Travis hands me his phone, and I read his texts from Wilder reassuring us that she is fine and sleeping. I hand his phone back and scoot over to the middle seat. I just want to cuddle with him. I want to feel safe. I know that I was on the winning side with that guy, but I am also a woman and I want to feel protected by my man.

I spot a diner. "Shall we get some breakfast?" I ask him and he grins. He pulls into the parking lot, and I climb out his side. We sit beside each other in the booth. The diner is filled with drunk people and truckers. Travis and I are neither.

"You feeling okay?" he asks.

"Yeah, I'm fine. I was just worried for Joslyn. I feel like she has been through some things, and my momma bear instincts came out."

"You did the right thing, Momma." He kisses my temple and helps me open the menu.

"Gabby is going to freak when she sees my cast."

He laughs. "She will, but not as much as she will if she finds out she may have a sibling cooking."

I have to roll my eyes at that. "She or he is not a turkey roasting in the oven, Travis." He does that smirk thing that makes me want to jump his bones, but that will have to wait until we are home.

The waiter comes and we order our food: a huge platter of hash browns, eggs, toast, etc. "I already asked Aiden if he would stay with Gabby tomorrow when we go to the doctor," Travis says. "I figured you didn't want her to know yet."

Shock rings through me. He is always so thoughtful and it still shocks me. From the very beginning it's just been me, and now it's not. "Every single day I fall more and more in love with you."

He cups my jaw, kissing me softly. The kiss is filled with so much passion and love. It's like he is making love to me with a kiss, right here in the middle of the diner, but we are in our own world--others have not noticed.

thirteen

Bailey

Travis and I look at the little bean on the monitor and listen to the sound of our baby's heartbeat.

"It's real," I whisper to myself. All of it is finally sinking in. One part of me was afraid to think I was pregnant. Sometimes I talk myself out of believing this is real life. How can life be this good? I love someone in a way I thought only existed in books, but it's real and right here in front of me.

I've changed so much. When I first got here, I was so anxiety ridden. Travis made me realize that the little things don't matter. I just need to let things go and live in the moment.

He has made me so happy. I was happy before—don't get me wrong—but this is a different kind of happy. It has filled my heart to the brim. I still worry, though—what would happen if I lost him?

Travis's eyes haven't left the monitor.

"How far along am I?" I ask the obstetrician.

"Around four weeks," she says.

"So fucking tiny," Travis whispers, touching my flat tummy.

Aiden is in the waiting room with Gabby, distracting her, while Reid is being seen by another doctor. I happened to notice all of the women in the room staring at him like they're smitten. I can't wait for the day he falls hard for someone. He deserves that. He took Reid, and most men couldn't even fathom the idea.

"Here is a prescription for your prenatal vitamins, and stop at the front desk to make your next appointment." The doctor stands up and hands me a piece of paper and the prescription. "On this piece of paper is my cell phone number in case you ever need me ASAP."

She leaves the room and I change back into the sundress that I am wearing today. My hair is in loose barrel curls, my makeup is light, and I am wearing a pair of cute sandals. Gabby is in a sundress similar to mine, and her hair is curled too.

When we return to the waiting room, Gabby is fast asleep against Aiden's side. He has her covered with one of Reid's blankets. He is like the brother I always wanted, if I really think about it.

Travis rushes over to him and hands him the picture of our baby. Aiden takes it and grins. "Congrats man, happy for you." Travis is beaming. Reid thrusts his little leg out and kicks Gabby, waking her up.

She looks at me and then Travis. "Time to leave?" she says sleepily.

"Yes, sweetheart, you hungry?" I push her hair out of her face. She nods and lifts her arms toward Travis, and he picks her up. He has her so spoiled already.

"Thanks, Daddy." Her eyes widen at her slip, and then she shakes her head. "I meant Ravis."

Travis looks like a deer in headlights; then he snaps out of it and smiles at her with such emotion. "Don't sweat it, angel, you can call me whatever you want." She doesn't say anything, but I am more than happy with that response.

"Bye Aiden, see you soon." I take Travis's hand and walk out of the clinic. My mind is reeling after what just happened. It seems like an honest mistake, but I don't think it is. How could she not have started to see him as a father figure? He is with her all day, takes her to practice, takes care of her, and is there for her like a father would be. Not just any father, an incredible one. I squeeze his hand. I want him to know that everything is okay. Part of me thinks I should be panicking that she is getting so attached, but he is Travis.

He puts her in her seat, and I stand outside the truck with him, knowing he needs to speak to me. He runs his hand over the top of his head. He looks nervous for the first time since I met him. "Travis."

He finally looks at me. "She called me Daddy, Bailey. That hit me right here." He puts his hand over his chest, and I put my hand over his.

"Travis, you have been a dad to her since the moment you met her. You have been there for everything."

He looks at me, letting my words sink in. "I want her to be mine. I think of her as my daughter. I want to be with her through every step of her life. It doesn't matter if she is mine biologically, she is fucking mine."

He hesitates before saying, "I want to adopt her. I want her to be officially mine. She is mine in my heart, but I want that shit documented."

"I would love that, Travis. Her dad signed his rights over, so it won't be an issue." I don't even care if this seems too soon. Even if, for some horrible reason, we don't work out, I still want him to be a part of her life. He smiles, and I can see the weight of the world has been lifted off his shoulders. I realize that this has been bothering him quite a bit, and I am just glad he has some peace of mind.

Gabby loves him—she thinks the world revolves around him—and if I denied her this, what kind of parent would I be?

"I want to talk to her about it first," he says, "to see if she wants it." This is why he is perfect.

Travis

For the third time since meeting Gabby and Bailey, my world changed in a split second.

First was coming to realize that I loved them both, so fucking much. They stole a part of me the moment I met them. Second was finding out that Bailey was pregnant. Third was Gabby accidentally calling me Daddy; that shit hit me like a ton of bricks, right to my soul. My first thought was that I wanted to hear that every single day of my life. I want her to be officially mine, and I want to make sure she is okay with the idea. I want to get her thoughts on it. She is five years old, but she is intelligent enough to kind of understand what is happening.

At least Bailey is okay with it. I was scared of what her reaction would be. What if she told me no? I'm just in my fucking head; I knew better. Now it's time to talk to Gabby.

I am fucking nervous. Beyond nervous—I am a wreck. I am sitting on the floor in Gabby's room playing with her.

"Angel, can I talk to you?" I hold my breath waiting for her to look at me.

"Yes, Ravis." She scoots closer to me, giving me her full attention. So fucking smart for her age.

"Do you remember when you called me Daddy earlier?" Her eyes widen. "No baby, don't be scared. I just want to ask you something." I grab her small hand and smile at her, trying to ease her worries. "Do you want me to be your dad?" She doesn't say anything for a few seconds, before she nods. I close my eyes, overcome with emotion, and I pull her into my lap and just hug her. I open my eyes and look at her. "Good, I want you to be my daughter. You don't have to call me Dad if you don't want to. It's totally up to you."

She nods. "I think I would like to call you that. You and Mommy are together, so that makes you my daddy, so I would like to call you that. Right?" So fucking smart, way beyond her years.

I kiss the top of her head. "I would love that, angel." I take out my phone and give Lane the go-ahead. We have deep connections. We are getting a judge to draw up the papers, as we speak, and they will be here later today. That is technically illegal, but when everyone's in your pocket it's easier to get things done. Why would I wait? They are what I want.

Gabby climbs out of my lap and goes back to playing, not realizing the impact she just had on my life. Bailey is standing at the door, watching us. My life has changed so much since I met her. Everything has changed. I have a family. My world never started until I saw them get off the plane. I stumbled and almost fell on my ass and I knew, in that instant, when their eyes hit mine.

fourteen

Bailey

I laugh as Gabby runs across the beam at the park. Travis is clenching his hands. She jumps and, as he runs to catch her, she lands gracefully.

"I'm about to panic," Travis tells me and I burst out laughing again. I understand the feeling.

"You should have seen me when she was jumping off of tables, doing flips."

He shakes his head. "I think it's best we wrap her in bubble wrap before she ends up with a broken wrist like her momma."

"Ha, ha, ha," I say. "Want me to break my other one?" I tease him.

He holds his hands up in mock surrender, taking a step back.

"You better step back, if you know what's good for you."

His eyes flash with laughter, and he crosses his arms and gives me a look, daring me to do something about it.

"Ravis, help me reach the bars," Gabby calls, jumping up and down to reach the monkey bars. He runs over and lifts her up. I sit down on the bench, press my hand to my stomach, and close my eyes, reveling in the sound of Gabby's laughter. Travis is encouraging her and cheering her on. Everything is just perfect.

"Bailey," someone says.

I open my eyes, and I can't believe who is standing next to me. Randall. My stomach hits the floor, and I immediately feel ill. I stand up and back away, putting distance between us. He grins at me. It's not a genuine one; that's for sure. Chills are running up my spine, and I just want to run away. I look over at Gabby, who is still playing. "What are you doing here, Randall?"

Travis jumps up and I swallow hard. I don't want Gabby to see Randall.

"I just wanted to come see you and *my* daughter. I got a call from the insurance company letting me know that our daughter was sick."

I just laugh. "*Our* daughter? You mean..."

Travis stands beside me, facing Randall head-on, and finishes my sentence. "Our daughter." He takes my hand, and I know that he wants me to be strong, to stand up to Randall.

"You gave up your rights, Randall," I tell him. "You have no ties to either of us."

His fake smile drops in a split second. "That doesn't fucking matter. She is my daughter, and I am going to get her right now." The sound of that familiar angry snarl makes me flinch.

"Watch your fucking tone, before I make you eat your words," Travis snarls right back, getting closer to Randall. If looks could kill, Randall would have been dead ten times over by now.

His eyes widen; I guess he is not used to being talked back to. Then I realize Randall is not scary anymore. When I first saw him, all of those old instincts came back at the sound of his voice.

"Want to bet? I bet she will run right to me." Randall starts in Gabby's direction.

Travis reaches out and grabs his shoulder. "Take another fucking step, I will blow your fucking brains out." I shiver at the tone of his voice.

Randall does the dick thing and yells, "Gabby! Baby, come to daddy!" Why is he such a cruel person?

She finally walks over and sees Randall. She shakes her head, and I motion for her to come to me. That's when I notice three guys approaching her from the opposite side of the park.

"Travis." My stomach hits the ground as they get closer and closer to Gabby. Travis runs toward them. As I start to follow him, an arm bands around my waist and I am lifted off the ground. Another man is holding me, with Randall right beside him. "Let's go!" Randall roars.

"Let me go!" I scream, kicking and punching. I lean forward and then bring my head back, as hard as I can, and I hear a crack as the back of my head connects with his face. He loosens his grip, and my feet hit the ground.

Randall smiles before his fist connects with the side of my face. Right before everything goes black, I see Travis fighting off six men. He looks at me with panic and then continues to fight, and Gabby is running across the field.

Travis

I will never fucking forget her expression before the fucker punched her right in the face, a fucking van pulled up beside her, and Randall threw her inside.

Now they are gone. Anger hits me so fucking hard I can taste it. "Run baby," I tell Gabby. I need her as far away as possible while I finish this. These are the same men who Bailey's mom hired. They are wearing the exact same clothes, and the tattoos on their forearms are the same. I take out my gun; luckily, I have a silencer on it.

I look back to make sure Gabby isn't looking; then I take the safety off and shoot the guy in front on the knee. He hits the ground. I kick him hard in the face. A fist moves toward me, and I duck and hit him with my elbow.

I raise my gun and pull the trigger again and again, in quick succession. All but two of the men hit the ground. One of them charges me. I am out of bullets, so I take out my knife, spin it, and plant it right in his fucking neck. The other fucker tries to run off, so I pull the knife out of the man's throat and throw it, hitting him in the back of the head. They are all down around me.

"Gabby!" I yell and run in the direction I saw her go. She comes out of a tunnel on the playground and runs to me, her legs moving so fast that she falls against me. I catch her and sprint to my truck with her tucked against my chest.

I put her in the truck, buckling her as fast as I can, and get in. I press the panic button on my phone and I am immediately ringed into Lane.

"What happened?" Lane asks, his voice deadly calm.

"They got her," I choke out. I am covered in blood and other shit, and Gabby is in the back seat crying, fucking breaking me. "There were six of them. Gabby is with me, but they got Bailey. Clean-up crew needed in the park, and I am coming to the club. I'm three minutes out." I hang up. I look in the rearview mirror and see Gabby rubbing her eyes. "You're safe, everything is fine."

Her bottom lip trembles. "Why did he take Mommy?"

Fuck me, that shit is going to fucking haunt her. It's going to haunt me, seeing her eyes roll back in her head as the fucker knocked her out. He is going to die, and he is not going to die easy. He will pay for every fucking sin.

"You're going to go see baby Reid, and I'm going to go get her, okay?" I say, and her eyes connect with mine in the mirror.

"Okay, Ravis. Hurry, okay?" Her faith in me makes me so fucking happy. I will not fail her, and I will not fail Bailey.

How the fuck did six men come out of nowhere? I know they had planned to take either Bailey or Gabby.

The clubhouse comes into view, and the gate is opened for me immediately. I pull the truck to a stop and take out Gabby. Adeline emerges in a split second. "Hey, sweet girl, want to go play with Reid and Noah?" She looks at me and I nod. I hug Gabby tightly, my eyes stinging. I hate this fucking shit. I should have taken Bailey with me when I went for Gabby. I could have done a million other fucking things differently, but I have to live with that. "I love you, angel baby."

"I love you too, Daddy." I close my eyes and kiss the top of her head before handing her over to Adeline.

Lane, Aiden, Wilder, Smiley, Konrad, Walker, Tristan, and Xavier walk up to me. "We have tracked her GPS on her phone. Let's ride. Travis, we already brought a spare of yours out." After I reload my gun, I climb on my spare bike, and I calm down instantly because some fuckers are about to die today.

Lane takes off and I follow closely. We are breaking every law known to man, but I need to get to her. I need to make sure she is okay. If they fucking hurt her in any way, they will experience that tenfold before I end their fucking lives.

Ten minutes later, we stop outside a house right in the middle of fucking nowhere. It's convenient for us, though. Not as many people to hear their screams.

Xavier, Tristan, and Konrad run to the back to make sure they don't sneak out that way. I don't bother waiting for everyone else. I kick in the front door. Aiden is right by my side, and Lane, Wilder, and Smiley are right behind me. One fucker is sitting on the couch. I take out my gun and put a bullet in his throat. They are not getting an easy out if I can help it.

Another fucker runs out a door, and I wrap my hand around back of his head. I smash his head over and over into the kitchen table. I keep doing this until his face is completely smashed in and throw his body to the floor. Then I push open the only door that is closed. Randall is standing there with a gun pressed to Bailey's head.

Bailey

I wake up to someone smacking me in the face, and I open my eyes and come face-to-face with my worst nightmare: Randall. "Well, look who is finally awake." My stomach turns as everything that has happened sinks in; then another thought hits me. My unborn baby. *Calm yourself, you don't want to lose your baby.*

My poor angel, Gabby. She fucking probably saw me being taken, and I hope that she forgets it. And Travis...the look on his face was one of pure terror. I hope he doesn't blame himself. He was taking on at least six men at once. And all I care about is that he protected Gabby and got her out of that situation. I pray to God that she is with him.

"I need to strike a deal with you," Randall says, and I snort with laughter. Does he really think I am going to do that?

"What the fuck is so funny, bitch?" He grips my jaw hard, and I look him straight in the eyes.

"You. I am not afraid of you anymore." It's true. I am not afraid of him anymore. Not the way I used to be.

"Want to fucking bet? You will sign over all of your money, and if you don't, I will kill you and take Gabby." I laugh again. He smacks me hard across the face, and I look him straight in the eye again.

"Did you know Travis adopted Gabby? She is not yours, and she is a princess to the Grim Sinners MC, you will never touch her." I don't care. He is not going to rule my life anymore.

I hear the sound of a bunch of bikes pulling up outside, and he looks out the window. "How the fuck did they find you?" I hear the front door being broken in and I grin. *He is here for me.* He is okay—and I know Gabby is too, or he wouldn't be here.

Thump, thump, thump. Flesh is hitting something hard. Randall grabs me and presses the gun to my head. The door opens, and Travis is standing right here in front of me. He is covered in blood, but I don't think it's his.

"Why don't you face me like a real man," Travis says to Randall, who just presses the gun harder against my temple. You know what? I am tired of this shit. I grab his arm and push the gun away, just as he pulls the trigger. The bullet hits the ground.

Travis charges and tackles him to the ground, punching him over and over in the face. Minutes, seconds, or hours pass—I don't know; it's like I am having an out-of-body experience. Then Travis stops, and Randall groans.

"Aiden, drag him outside for me," Travis says.

Aiden grabs Randall's feet and takes him from the room. Travis falls to his knees in front of me, and the others leave the room, giving us privacy. I place my mouth to the back of his head, which is pressing against my belly. "Are you okay?" I ask him. He lets out a deep shaky breath before he looks at me. I touch the side of his face and rest my forehead against his.

"*Me?* Are you okay? Are you hurt? The baby?" He touches my stomach.

"He only hit me in the face, I am fine." Then I ask, in a high-pitched voice, "Gabby?"

"She is fine, she is at the club with Adeline. I don't think she saw much." I sink back in my chair.

Travis stands up and kisses me softly on the lips. "I need to go do something, baby. Walker will stay here with you, and then we are going home." I nod, closing my eyes. I know what he needs to do. "Love you, Momma."

I smile for the first time since this shit went down. "I love you too, make him pay." There is no remorse on my side, not after I was fucking kidnapped and Gabby and my unborn child were put in danger. There's no going back from that.

Travis

Randall is sitting, leaning against the house, when I walk outside. Lane, Wilder, Smiley, and Aiden are in front of him, taunting him. Randall scoots back when he sees me. That's right, fucker, you need to be fucking prepared.

"Wait, did you know that bitch in there is a millionaire? Why the fuck aren't you doing the same thing I am?" Randall says as if it's the most realistic thing on Earth.

"So are we, fucker. She is not the only one with money."

Lane laughs, and Randall's eyes widen. That's right, fucker. There's no getting out of this one.

"I am going old school on this one. Who wants to help me to do the fucking honors?" I ask.

Wilder steps forward. "I will." Aiden runs over to the bikes and takes out a pair of chains. I pull Randall's legs, and his head hits the ground.

"Ouch, what the fuck is your problem?"

I bend over and grab his throat. "My fucking problem started when Bailey was seventeen years old. You got her pregnant and didn't do shit but make her life hell." I tighten my grip on his throat. "She fucking starved, she went hungry, and you would come over and eat in front of her. You fucking treated her like shit beneath your feet." His eyes widen. *Good, motherfucker, you're about to die and it's going to be long, hard, and painful.* "My daughter, you abandoned her. You fucking called her mother names. You called her names, and you kidnapped her mother in front of her. You don't deserve to be alive another fucking second." I just want to choke the life out of him, but that would be too easy.

"Let's not forget I paid the worker when she was climbing the rock wall."

I lock eyes with Lane, and I work my jaw and stand up, grinding Randall's hand under my foot. He screams and I hear the snap of his hand breaking.

Aiden hands me the chain, and I wrap it around his legs. I give a sharp pull to make sure it's going to stay. I leave him lying there, and I walk over to my bike. Wilder is already on his. We hook one chain to my bike and the other to Wilder's. I nod and we both take off at the same time, dragging Randall behind us. He screams and I grin. He had choices in life. He could have been a good fucking human being, and he didn't choose that route, and now it's time to drag out the trash. Justice is being served.

We drag him until he is quiet; then we ride back to the house. Lane checks Randall for a pulse. "Dead," he mouths to me.

I turn off my bike and stare down at the corpse. I hope you enjoy hell, fucker. I hope the fucking torment continues beyond the grave and never ends.

"I will move him." Smiley takes off the chains and drags him behind the building so Bailey won't see him, but there's no way she won't see the bloodstains on the ground.

The front door opens and she steps out. She comes right to me and rests her head on my chest. I nod at Walker, who stayed with her.

"We will handle everything, go home and rest," Lane tells me. I climb on my bike and Bailey gets on behind me, hugging my back tightly. "Ready?"

"More than ready."

fifteen

Bailey

Later That Night

We are all in bed, freshly showered and relaxing, cuddling and watching a movie. Gabby is already back to her happy-go-lucky self.

She was so excited to see me, and the first thing she said was, "I knew Ravis would get you." If Travis's smile was anything to go by, that made him feel like he was a million feet tall.

"Gabby, you know what to do," Travis says and I arch my eyebrows, confused. I touch my belly, waiting to see what they're up to. Gabby comes back and Travis comes around to my side of the bed. He takes my hand and pulls me out of the bed. "Thank you, angel." He takes something from Gabby's hand. Travis looks at me, a small

195

smile tugging at his lips, "Fuck, this is probably not the best time for this, but after what happened today, what is?"

I blink, confused, as he gets down on one knee before me; then it slowly starts to sink in what is happening. I put my hand over my mouth, already fighting tears.

"Momma, I love you so much. You brought me the most precious gifts of my life: your heart and Gabby's. You stole my heart the second I saw you get off of that plane. I knew in that very second that you guys were mine, and my life was never the same." He grips my left hand, pressing the ring against my ring finger. "I never knew what living actually was until you. I never knew I was missing parts of my heart until you guys fixed it. Then, for the first time in my life, I actually breathed."

Tears are rolling down my face, and my heart feels like it's going to explode. "Will you do me the honor and marry me?"

"YES!" I scream, and he puts the ring on my finger. I wrap my arms around his neck, tackling him, and press kisses all over his face. He laughs and Gabby cheers. Life is just perfect. They're perfect.

epilogue

A Couple of Months Later

"You ready, angel?" I ask Gabby. She is standing beside me before we walk down that aisle, where Travis will be waiting for us.

I am around six months pregnant. This is not how I expected my wedding to go, but I couldn't have pictured a better one.

"Yes." Gabby grins. She is missing one of her front teeth, and she is so adorable. The last couple of months have been among the best. We finally got into a routine and found peace. My mother is already married to someone else and playing mommy to his kids. I feel sorry for them because of their witch of a stepmother.

Gabby takes my hand, and we wait for the doors to open. When they do, the first thing I see is Travis, but he is not where I expected him to be. He is standing right inside the doors, not at the altar. His presses his hand over his mouth as he looks me up and down, fire burning in his eyes; then he looks down at Gabby and his eyes soften. "My girls are beautiful."

We step closer to him, and he takes my hand and hers. "You guys will never have to walk alone again, that includes down the aisle." He is just perfect. He knew today was hard on me because I didn't have anyone to walk me down the aisle.

I wish I had a father, one that I could share this moment with, but I know Gabby will have an amazing, loving father, and that is what's important. He shows me and Gabby every single day that he loves us. We got lucky on so many levels, and today is the day I become Mrs. Chambers. I will be his in every single way, and today Gabby is getting her name changed also.

"You girls ready?" he asks.

"Ready."

"Ready, Daddy."

Together we walk down the aisle with our friends and family surrounding us. It is another beginning in an unending journey to being an ole lady to the Grim Sinners MC.

Three years later

Bailey

"It's finally here." Travis stands next to me in the circle of the houses I have built. They form a small community of their own.

It took three long years, but it's here. My dream is becoming a reality. Travis is holding our son, Gage. He is a mommy's boy through and through, that's for sure. Gabby is all Travis's but he is mine. I take great satisfaction in the fact that he wants me all the time. Travis grumbles about it, but Gabby practically abandoned me once Travis came along. What's fair is fair, right?

Gabby is sitting in front of us with a little boy, who wandered up to the stage next to her. Gabby is now seven years old, and that hurts. I want her to stay a little baby forever, but I know that's not possible. We can dream, right?

Over the years she has gotten better and better at gymnastics. She is at a new gym and is exceeding their expectations.

Travis moves up to me, staring intently at Gabby and the little boy. The boy pushes a piece of her hair over her shoulder, and I cover my mouth so I don't laugh. "Is he flirting with her?" he whisper yells to me. I don't answer. I just watch Travis's heart being wrecked. Gabby looks over at him and gives him that smile, the one that will knock you straight on your butt.

"Gabriella LeAnn Chambers," Travis calls, and she looks back, her eyes widening at being caught.

"What, Daddy?" she says in that oh-so-sweet voice. She is so rotten, and it's all his fault.

"Don't *daddy* me, what did I tell you?"

"Daddy, he just said I was pretty!" she fake whines and I laugh at that. It's so funny to see Travis's downfall being a seven-year-old girl.

"I know…that's the problem," he grumbles under his breath.

"Travis, just wait until she's older."

He glares at me. "Don't say that shit to me. She is to never to have a boyfriend or anything along those lines." Oh, I bet that is going to go over well. I take Gage from Travis and snuggle him. Yes, he's almost three years old, but he's still my baby. I decided that two was enough for me. Maybe down the line we'll have more, but with Gabby's gymnastics and my center I just don't have the time.

My assistant waves at me from the bottom of the stage. Travis takes Gage and it's go time.

I stand behind the microphone and smile at the crowd below me. "Thank you, everyone, for being here today. It's been a long three years, and the day is here to finally open this place, which holds a special part of my heart." Gabby hugs my leg and I press my hand to the top of her head. "I got pregnant at seventeen." I tell them my story, explaining that, at one point, I was ashamed of the struggle I'd been through, but not anymore. I want to be a voice for other young girls, conveying the message that others struggle too, but we can make it through everything.

After my speech is over, I take the large scissors and cut the rope. Travis comes up and hugs me. "So fucking proud of you, Momma."

"Thank you for encouraging me, pushing me to be the best I can be." Without him I am not sure this would have been possible.

We have a kid-free evening, so the moment we get through the door to our house, I start ripping my clothes off.

Travis throws me over his shoulder and runs up the stairs, and I laugh and smack his ass.

"Momma, don't make redden your ass for that shit." I just do it again, but harder. I am tossed on the bed, and I bounce and crawl away from him. He grabs my legs and twists me over onto my stomach.

He starts with my calves, biting then soothing each sting with a lick. I shiver in anticipation. I know most couples say their sex life dies down after the kids, but it's the exact opposite for us. "Hungry for me, Momma?" He spreads my legs open, kissing between my thighs.

My legs shake as I try to bring myself closer to his mouth. "Always."

Smack! His hand lands on my ass, and I jolt at the pain before groaning. It just sets me on fire more. One second I am lying on the bed, fisting the sheets, and the next I am straddling his face. "Oh god," I moan, gripping the top of the headboard. Travis moves me as he wants, and I just hang on for the ride. My body freezes as he slides his thumb in my ass, and I come hard.

He flips me over so I am lying on my back. He smiles at me. He is sweet—that is something he can rarely stray from. Gage is exactly like Travis. Both of them are total sweethearts, but boy do they have tempers. He grips my thighs, spreading my legs so he can fit between them, and I lean up to kiss him, my hands pressed against his face.

He slides in and I break the kiss, tilting my head back. I press my hands against the headboard as he slides out and back in, hard. I slide up the mattress a bit and hold on a little longer. "That's right, Momma, hold on." He bites the side of my neck before he pounds into me, and I bite my lip so I don't scream. Smack! I look at him. "What did I tell you about keeping that in? I want to hear all of you."

He circles my clit with his thumb; then he tilts and changes his angle. I come hard, once again, and wrap my legs around him as he moves harder and harder. "One more time," he demands.

I shake my head. "I can't," I whisper. His thumb strokes my oversensitive clit, and I scream—it's too much, in the best possible way—and then I fall apart again and he joins with me.

As he slides out of me, he presses his hand against my pussy. "Mine," he says and I laugh. He is such an alpha male. He leans on an elbow, grinning at me. "You ready for round two?"

I wink. "When am I not?"

Eleven Years Later

"Go Gabby!" I scream when she is on the high beam, and she flashes all of us a grin. She is doing everything absolutely perfectly.

Gage is sitting beside me, ignoring the girls trying to flirt with him. He is thirteen years old, but he is such a beautiful boy and looks older than his years. He is straight Travis, right down to his personality.

Gage is only concerned about one girl, and that's Aubree, Aiden's daughter, much to Aiden's chagrin. Grace and I enjoy teasing him about it too.

"That's my girl!" Travis yells as Gabby sticks the landing. Did I mention we are at the Olympics in a foreign country? My baby girl, at eighteen years old, is in her first Olympics. I'm so proud of her. She has dedicated herself to this for years.

I hold my breath as she flips off the beam, and I look at the screen as she gets a perfect score. I scream, jumping up and down. Gabby does the same and her teammates run over, hugging her.

"Damn, look at the legs on her," a man behind us says. In sync Travis's and Gage's heads snap around to glare at him.

"Better avert your eyes if you want to keep them," Travis says and Gage nods. Like I said, they are identical.

"She did it, Travis." I watch her receive a first-place medal over and over again.

"She did, baby. She is going to go far in life."

"She already has." She is accomplishing her dreams. She never stopped because it was hard, and it *was* hard on her. We encouraged her to be the best she can be, to never give up.

Her goal is to eventually open her very own gym in our town. She is going to college and has so many goals in life. Much to Travis's relief, guys haven't really been on her radar, but I can't wait for the day that it actually does happen and she meets her guy. I just wonder who he will be.

Later: She did find her guy. And boy, were we surprised.

Next we will be getting Aiden and Grace!

acknowledgements

To my readers. Without you this journey wouldn't be happening. Thank you from the bottom of my heart.

Lydia, thank you for everything you do for me. Without you, half of what needs to be done wouldn't be.

To my Devil and Grim girls, thank you for your unwavering support. I love you guys.

AUTHOR LINKS

Page: https://www.facebook.com/Author-Teagan-Wilde-2112786585717655/
Facebook Reader Group:
https://www.facebook.com/groups/1163716090445778/
My email is: authorleannashers@gmail.com (Feel free to email me! I love to hear your thoughts!)

My Social Media's under LeAnn Ashers
Facebook: https://www.facebook.com/LeAnnashers
Instagram: https://www.instagram.com/leann_ashers/
Twitter: https://twitter.com/LeannAshers
Goodreads:
https://www.goodreads.com/author/show/14733196.LeAnn_A
shers

LeAnn Asher's is a blogger turned author who released her debut novel early 2016 and can't wait to see where this new adventure takes her. LeAnn writes about strong-minded females and strong protective males who love their women unconditionally.

Facebook Page: www.facebook.com/Leannashers
Twitter: @LeannAshers
Email: Authorleannasher@gmail.com

More from LeAnn Ashers

Forever Series

Protecting His Forever
Loving His Forever

Devil Souls MC Series

Torch
Techy
Butcher
Liam

Grim Sinners MC Series

LeAnn Ashers

Lane
Wilder
Smiley

This series is under my paranormal pen name
Teagan Wilde

Raleigh Texas Wolves
<u>Damon</u>